For the Love of Money

Wilburta Arrowood

Publishing Designs, Inc.
Huntsville, Alabama

Publishing Designs, Inc.
P.O. Box 3241
Huntsville, Alabama 35810

Printed in the United States

Library of Congress Cataloging-in-Publication Data

Arrowood, Wilburta, 1943-
  For the love of money / Wilburta Arrowood.
    p. cm.
  ISBN 978-0-929540-69-6 (alk. paper)
  1. Men with disabilities—Fiction. 2. Compulsive gamblers—Fiction. I. Title.

PS3601.R724F67 2008
813'.6—dc22
                                    2008001040

Chapter One

*E*d Johnson slammed the checkbook on the desk and rubbed his hand across his face. His eighteen-month-old son, Desmond, jumped and began to cry. Ed groaned, aware he should have been better controlled. He leaned over and patted the boy and handed him a toy. "It's okay, son. Your daddy's just a little frustrated right now."

Desmond's pearly little teeth gleamed through the broad grin on his chocolate-colored face before he took the squeaky dog and began to chew on an ear. Ed was thankful it hadn't taken much to appease the baby.

He wished it could be so easy to solve his own problems. There just wasn't enough money for all the bills. Even with his wife, Kathy, working two jobs, and his own new job, the bills still threatened to overwhelm them at any moment. If only he hadn't been shot last summer, or if he had recovered sooner, or if he weren't confined to this cumbersome wheelchair for the rest of his life. Unfortunately, wishes made nothing change. He would always be crippled, and his hospital bills would not go away.

Ed knew he should be grateful for the job he'd been trained to do since the accident. If it weren't for Bruce Jacobson and his insistence that Ed could do the job if he would just try, no telling where he and Kathy would be by now. Bruce was a good Christian man, and he had certainly been good to Ed and Kathy, as well as many other people, but his generosity didn't extend far enough to bail Ed and Kathy out of their current financial mess.

Kathy stepped into their small living room where Ed's desk stood near a front window. Kathy had insisted it needed to be there while Ed was recuperating so he could watch the world outside. "What's all the banging around about?" she asked as she dried her hands on a towel.

Ed knew the kitchen would be spotless by now, and soon Kathy

3

would go to bathe Desmond and put him to bed. It frustrated Ed even more that he couldn't even do a simple task like that anymore. Kathy had so much of the load to carry, many things he used to handle, but was no longer able to do.

"I'm just going over the bills. We're short again this month—and don't you even think about asking for any more overtime. You're already workin' sixty hours a week between your two jobs. You're gonna collapse if you keep that up, and then where'll we be?"

Kathy came and laid her arm across his shoulder and glanced down at the checkbook and the stack of bills beside it. "Who can we put off? I can call and explain our situation. Most people will be patient if they know what's happening, and that we do intend to pay. If only they will just give us a little more time."

Ed shook his head and let the scowl deepen on his brow. "That might help with the ones we haven't already talked to. What about the ones who are already waiting; and what happens next month? It won't be any better then. We have to come up with something long-term."

Kathy sighed, sank onto a nearby chair, and sat silent for a long moment. When she did speak, Ed wanted to cry. Of course, he wouldn't do that. Real men didn't cry. Not ever. Especially not men who had been through all the things he'd endured already.

"Ed, there are banks that will consolidate debts. Maybe if we went to one, they would help us consolidate everything into one loan and set up one payment over a longer period of time to get us a little bit of breathing space." Kathy leaned over to lift Desmond from the walker.

Ed shook his head. "You know better than that, Kathy. Who's going to loan that much money to an ex-con?" She looked so weary. Ed wanted to go to her and smooth the frown wrinkles from her face and hold her hands in assurance. He wanted to pull her into his lap and kiss her down-turned lips into the beautiful smile he remembered from months before. She tried so hard to do all the things he couldn't, and she did most of them and handled it well, but some things she simply could not do. Erasing his past was one of those things. They had been treated so kindly at church these past couple of years that Kathy forgot what it could be like in the real world. The world where people didn't forget the mistakes a person had made. The world where they kept score for your entire lifetime. The world where nobody believed you could repent and change—but rather that you could only continue to perpetuate other offenses.

Ed knew the church members where he and Kathy attended had forgiven him his past—the past where he killed the minister's wife several years ago—and he knew that same minister truly forgave and loved Ed and his family. But he also knew the general public and business world were not so forgiving. Ed's record would keep him from getting any help from a bank, or probably even from any of the loan shops that charge outrageous interest. No, the only people who could get loans were those who were rich enough that they didn't really need them.

Desmond began to cry again and Kathy rose. "I'll go give him his bath. He'll want to go to bed soon."

Ed nodded and turned back to the stack of bills, intent on finding one or more they could put on hold for a few weeks. The problem was, everything here had to be paid, or they would not be able to continue to live in their small home. When they first looked at the house, Kathy was pregnant and they had saved for a couple of years for the down payment. Ed didn't understand just how, but the real estate agent had worked some sort of special financing through the government so they could get the loan. Ed remembered how proud they had been when they moved in. It wasn't the biggest house in the world, but it met their needs. It would have been nice to have another bathroom, and Kathy would have enjoyed a larger kitchen, and the bedroom was barely large enough to walk between the bed and the dresser. But it was their own home and it was all they could afford when they first bought it. Now it was more than they could afford, but moving was not an option. Even a smaller apartment would cost more per month than their house payment.

Living here presented several problems. Kathy now had to be responsible for all the lawn care. She had to do, or arrange to have done, all the minor repair jobs. Oh, Ed supervised, and handed her tools, and gave her a hand with anything he could reach from his chair, but that didn't amount to much. When the water heater quit working last month, Kathy and Ed spent several hours in the basement removing the burner and cleaning it.

Since they owned the house, they had to pay all the utility bills. The only thing their payment covered was the house loan and the insurance policy the loan company insisted they carry. Ed contemplated having the phone removed, but he knew he couldn't do that. He needed the modem for his job. He and Kathy had already quit making any long-distance calls, so all they had was their basic charge, and Ed's boss paid for the monthly Internet service, so Ed couldn't complain about that. The water bill was minimal, as was the gas bill. The electricity bill was outrageous, especially since they weren't home in the day. What could he do to cut that? He couldn't think of anything they weren't already doing.

He and Kathy always turned the lights off when they left a room. They used fans instead of air conditioning, and only in the rooms that were occupied. That left a lot to be desired, but it wasn't unbearable. After all, for hundreds of years people hadn't even heard of air conditioning. They would survive, although Ed knew it made things harder for Kathy. Desmond fussed more, and that made more work for his mother, and when she held the baby she was even hotter. Anger boiled up in Ed's chest.

Why did God let that maniac shoot him last summer? Why did he let it paralyze Ed from the waist down? Didn't God think the ten years Ed spent in prison for Cora Forrest's death was enough punishment? If not, why didn't he just let Ed stay in prison instead of sending Micah to teach him about God and his Son? If Micah hadn't done that, Ed would probably have spent the rest of his life in prison. Instead he'd been released after Micah pleaded for him. Ed had grown hopeful of a new life in service to God, and he'd married Kathy. Kathy, the love of his life, and the helpmate of his faith; Kathy, the mother of his child, and the backbone of their future as strong Christians.

Ed slammed his fist on the checkbook again. What kind of God would let him see what life could be like and then snatch it back? Certainly not the loving God Micah talked about. The God Ed knew was cruel—more cruel than he had ever imagined.

Chapter 2

As soon as he finished his meager dinner, Ed returned to his desk. It startled him when the doorbell rang, and he wheeled his chair over to unlatch the screen door. When he swung it open, his brother LaMont stood on the porch, sporting a toothy grin.

"Yo, Bro. What's happenin'?" the lanky brown teen asked as he stepped into the room. He clasped his huge dark hands in front of him and cracked his knuckles in nonchalant abandon, just short of strutting in his baggy pair of bright red silky gym shorts, a black tank top, and high-topped tennis shoes. The black wooly hair protruding in numerous knots all over his head shouted, "Cool."

"Nothin' good," Ed mumbled before he pulled the screen door shut and latched it again. "What you doin' here?"

"I just stopped by to see if you were good and bored yet. Thought we might play some cards, or somethin'." LaMont dropped onto the lumpy brown sofa and sprawled across the entire length.

Ed wondered when the boy would ever quit growing. LaMont's length served him well when he played basketball, and it helped him win a scholarship. To his disadvantage, it sure did make it hard for him to buy clothes. Ed looked at his brother's feet and thought he must wear a size ninety-nine! Ed was a big man, but nothing like his brother.

Ed turned back to the desk. "I don't think so, LaMont. I need to get some of these bills paid. Trouble is, there isn't enough money to go around." Ed had to get at least some of this under control. The stress was hard on him, and even worse, it wore at Kathy. Ed already wondered what kept Kathy here with him. He couldn't even do simple chores around the house any more. Kathy had it all on her shoulders.

"So," LaMont drawled, "don't worry about it right now. If you don't have the money, you can't do nothin' 'bout 'em, and you might as well enjoy the evenin'."

Ed shook his head. He couldn't do that. He had to work to keep Kathy here. She'd never actually threatened to leave—in fact, she continually assured him she loved him and would always be here. That didn't keep Ed from worrying. He knew something as innocuous as dripping water would eventually wear a hole in a rock. His Kathy was more solid than stone, but even she would have a breaking point.

"Come on, Bro," LaMont coaxed. "You need a break. All that will be there when I leave, and you can tackle it then."

Ed knew there was something faulty with LaMont's reasoning, but he agreed he didn't see how he could do much with the bills, so he stuffed them into the desk drawer. "So what's your game, little brother?"

LaMont grinned broadly and sprang upright. "I thought we could play poker like we did when we were kids. You know, we used to play for matches, and you always went away with enough to start a fire the size of Montana, but I been practicing. You won't get that many from me anymore."

Ed laughed and wheeled his chair toward the kitchen table. "Get the cards out of that top desk drawer over there, and get ready to lose your shirt, little boy. I got you covered."

LaMont sauntered to the desk and pulled out a couple of decks and asked, "Matter which deck?"

"Yeah," Ed said, "the red ones. I feel mighty lucky tonight and red's my lucky color."

"Then you're in trouble, man. I got on *my* lucky red shorts." LaMont raised his arms above his head and did a silly spin in front of Ed. "Not a chance do you have."

Ed motioned to the chair across from where he sat. "Sit and deal and weep."

Each man laid five matches on the table before LaMont dealt the cards with a sure, swift flourish.

"High hand wins," LaMont said as he picked up his hand.

Ed nodded and gathered his cards. "You have been practicing. Used to you couldn't even get 'em shuffled good."

LaMont flashed another broad grin. "Told you."

Ed allowed himself to smile a tiny bit, even though he knew he had better luck if he used his long-practiced poker face. He discarded three cards and LaMont dealt him the replacements.

LaMont studied his own hand, discarded two, and took two new ones.

Ed bid five matches and waited.

LaMont eyed his cards longer than Ed could imagine any reason to do so. Eventually LaMont met the bet and upped it five, then leaned to turn his cards up on the table.

Ed chuckled, then exposed his own hand. "My full house beats your three of a kind."

LaMont shook his head. "Man, I just knew when you grinned you were tryin' to throw me off. You never used to let a muscle twitch even a tiny bit."

Ed gathered the cards to deal again. "Yeah, I'll have to work on that if I do much of this in the future."

"Well," LaMont said, "it ain't gonna be a problem if you're as broke as you say. You won't even be able to buy matches."

Ed frowned and spread the cards before them for another hand. "You're right there. As long as it's just you and me and we're playin' for matches maybe I won't get any more broke than I already am."

LaMont gathered his cards. "Sounds right to me."

Kathy stepped back into the room. "The kitchen is clean, so I'm going to put Desmond to bed, and then read a while."

"Good," Ed said. "You need a break. Enjoy your book."

Kathy laughed. "I don't know how enjoyable that thick training manual will be, but I have to get through it before Monday."

Ed scowled. "Can't you spend even an hour or so on a book of fiction and relax?"

"Not tonight," Kathy said. "I get too sleepy to read for very long, and I have my review interview on Monday."

Ed's hands fisted, and he had to force them down to prevent pounding the table. The water drops just kept pounding Kathy and he was powerless to stop them.

Kathy stooped and kissed Ed on the head. "Quit scowling. It's just a review. I already know that stuff—all I need is a quick reminder. If you guys stay out of my hair, I'll finish in no time."

"We can do that," LaMont said before he shuffled the cards again.

The two men continued to play for another couple of hours, and even though Ed lost a few hands, when the game ended, he had a broad stack of matches in front of him. LaMont had only nine. Ed still had his "magic" touch with the cards. His instinct was still good. He hadn't tried it recently. He just knew he could beat all his former opponents as well. He'd been awesome in his teens, and he felt that same surge of invincibility he'd felt after every one of those games. Poker was his game.

"I thought I had you." LaMont cocked his head and slid the stack of matches over to Ed. "If you hadn't had that queen, you'd have been in trouble. You won tonight, but I'll be back. You better work at keepin' your cool, man."

Ed shook his head. "Come on back anytime and deal, and duck."

LaMont dropped into the chair again. "I think I want to teach you a lesson right here and now, big brother." He shuffled the cards and proceeded to deal.

Kathy came back into the room and frowned. "Do you guys know what time it is?"

Ed glanced at his watch and saw it was after ten. "It's Friday. Nobody has to go to work tomorrow. What about you, LaMont? Any classes?"

"Not 'til mid-morning, and I'm not ready to let you dance off with all my matches."

Kathy looked at the little pile by Ed's hand. "You two aren't gambling, are you?"

Ed shook his head before he picked up the cards LaMont had just laid before him. "Nope, honey, we're just playing a little poker for matches. No money's exchangin' hands. We're just killin' time like we did when we were kids at home. I haven't lost my touch, either. I can still whip the tail off this big lunk."

"As long as you're just 'having fun,'" Kathy said.

Ed nodded, and didn't say anything. He liked beating LaMont. It was downright fun to see his baby brother brag and then have to back off. Ed liked the rush of winning, too. He'd always liked to play cards, and he and LaMont and even their mom had played for hours. It was something to do when there was no television and no other diversions they could afford to keep themselves entertained. Ed had loved whipping his brother and even his mother at the endless card games. He'd hoarded boxes of matches and got them out and stacked them on the table now and again, just to remind them of how good he was. In retrospection, he wondered why they kept playing with him. Of course, it was because there was nothing else to do, and even losing was better than sitting and studying the wallpaper.

LaMont folded his cards together and stood. "I have to go. I do have that mid-morning class tomorrow."

Ed watched his brother leave, then wheeled to the desk. He had to address at least part of the bills. He turned the computer on and pulled up the accounting program. He supposed the house payment was most pressing, and he could pay that online. He clicked on the Internet icon and waited for it to load. When he reached the mortgage company's site and keyed in his password, it took only a click to diminish his checking account to the point of near nonexistence. He left the secure site and went to his favorite game site. The usual pop-ups plagued him, and he started to click them closed before one caught his attention.

"Online poker games. Best on the net." It glittered with bold golds and greens and it had poker chips strewn around a green-felted table. Ed stared at it and let his mind skip around what he saw. It looked attractive, professional, not some fly-by-night operation. He was good at poker. Could this be a way to earn the money he needed?

He only entertained the thought a moment before he clicked the pop-up out of sight. No way could anybody beat a pre-programmed computer. He knew that much, but still . . .

Chapter 3

Kathy carried a wet, towel-encased Desmond to the living room and dropped onto a chair to dry and dress him for bed. She patted and blotted, and glanced over at Ed and bit her lip. Her husband was a good man, but he'd spent way too much time in prison with little to entertain him. She knew after Micah took an interest in Ed, her husband had spent most of his free time reading his Bible and trying to find the answers he'd missed so far. He'd made a complete change in his life, and now Kathy couldn't imagine a better man than her Ed anywhere on this earth. Kathy also knew that before Ed became a Christian, he had played poker for hours and hours with the other inmates. He'd told her how he had been dubbed King of Aces for his well-known skill at the game. Others talked about luck, but Ed believed it was a skill, and whichever it was, he had a definite knack for winning. He'd grown so good at it many of his fellow inmates refused to play with him. They were not eager to lose their smokes or their canteen money. None of them had access to very much, but Ed always managed to win whatever was available. He'd never smoked, but he bartered cigarettes for other things he needed or wanted.

Kathy watched when Ed's hand hesitated before he clicked off the pop-up on the computer screen advertising the online games. Worry pressed down on her. She let it enter her mind and skitter around. What if Ed started gambling for real? Ed was a strong Christian, and he took part in as many of the projects at church as he was able to handle. She didn't want anything to interfere with that. She realized their finances were in really bad shape, and she also knew gambling would make it worse. Even if Ed could win some of the time, the odds were definitely against him. He could not come out the ultimate winner. Anybody with half a brain should be able to see that.

She sighed in relief when Ed clicked on to a video game instead. Things were okay for now, but Kathy had an uneasy feeling about this sudden spurt of new interest in gaming, and she scolded herself for her suspicions. Ed deserved a little diversion. He had so many burdens to bear, especially now that he had to spend all his time in that horrid wheelchair. He had a right to a few moments of pleasure, and he and LaMont had not really been gambling after all. They had both used matches from Kathy's own kitchen. Neither of them owned the matches, so they could neither truly claim them at game's end, even if they had wanted to. She was making something sinister out of a simple game for a bit of fun.

Kathy fastened the last button on Desmond's pajamas and rose to carry him to his father for a good night kiss. "Here's your boy, Daddy."

Ed turned his chair around and she sat Desmond in Ed's lap.

"Man, you are getting heavy, kiddo," Ed exclaimed when he lifted his son to snuggle him on his shoulder.

"He's turned into a little eating machine," Kathy agreed. "A real meat-and-potatoes man." She grinned at father and son, and a rush of pride swept over her. The two of them shared the same dark brown coloring, the same sheared black wooly skullcap, and the same delicate long fingers. But most of all they shared the same sense of joy. They both laughed in an instant, over the most innocuous things. Even now, as Ed lifted Desmond over his head and lowered him swiftly, the little boy giggled uncontrollably in his high baby squeal, and Ed matched his son's squeals with a deep-toned adult mirth of his own.

Kathy stood back and watched the hilarity for a moment, then scolded, "You're gettin' him all riled up. I'll never settle him down enough to go to sleep."

Ed moved Desmond to one side just enough to look around him and meet Kathy's eyes. "Yes, you will. You're gonna sit right there in that rockin' chair and rock him until he does. And while you're rockin', you're gonna rest at least those few minutes."

Kathy shook her head. "I don't have time to sit that long. You may have to read him to sleep tonight. I still have laundry to do."

It surprised her when Ed sat Desmond back on his lap and snapped, "I don't want you workin' any more tonight. I want you to sit down and rest a few minutes."

She stood a moment and gazed deep into his eyes before she spoke softly. "Ed, I love you for your intent, but it isn't helping when you insist on something like this. It just puts me further behind, and later I have to work even harder to catch up. The best way you can help me right now is to read to Desmond and let me get on with my household business."

Ed glowered at her a long moment, and she thought he might refuse. Finally he nodded. "Hand me a couple of books."

Kathy went to the bookcase and pulled out *Goodnight, Moon,* and *Clifford The Big Red Dog.* When she crossed the room and handed them to her husband, her hand brushed his gently, and she purposely stroked the back of it again. "I'm sorry it's this way, Ed. I wish I could sit with you and Desmond and rock him to sleep every night, but you know I can't." She paused a moment, her hand lingering on his: "It won't be this way forever. Things will get better."

Ed took the book. "I guess, but I want it better now. I don't know how much longer you can go on workin' day and night, never takin' even a few minutes for yourself."

"I'm doin' just fine," she said before she turned and headed to the basement. She'd told Ed she was fine. In truth she was so weary she wasn't sure she would be able to climb back up that short span of stairs when it came time to go to bed.

She hung the clothes from the dryer and then moved another wet load to it. As she reloaded the washer, she puzzled how they were going to manage to meet all their bills. Didn't the creditors realize they could not squeeze blood out of a turnip? She and Ed might be able to sell the house, but they had only lived here a little over a year, and the equity was so small it would hardly touch their crisis. Besides, if they sold the house, where would they find anything any cheaper? No, moving wasn't the answer, but what was?

She picked up the basket of towels and undergarments she had dried earlier and hadn't had time to fold. She sank onto a folding chair in the "rec" room. It was a modest finished room, and it even had a kitchen stove, a sink, and a refrigerator at one end. The former owners had used the basement as a "mother-in-law" apartment. Kathy thought it must have been really depressing for anyone to have to spend all their time in such a small area. A few windows blinked around the upper perimeter of the room, so there was at least some natural light. Kathy supposed it would have been sufficient. It certainly couldn't be called cozy with the dark gold paint on the walls. Some day she would like to paint the whole basement white to make it more cheerful and bright. At least down here it was cooler than upstairs. They'd turned the air-conditioning off weeks ago and were only using fans because of the high electrical costs. It was easier to sleep with the heat than it was with the worry.

She started to work at the improvised folding table in the basement. She folded everything but the socks. Then as she sorted large, medium and small pieces by color and rolled them together, she prayed.

Lord, I don't know what to do. I don't want us to be deadbeats. I don't want us to lose our home. You've promised in your word that you'll take care of us, and I know that doesn't usually mean silk clothes and steak on the table, but we do need a place to live and some way to clothe Desmond. He's growing so fast, Lord, and even when I have time to shop the garage sales, it costs to keep up with him. Lord, I don't know what we're going to do. You're going to have to guide us in the right way to go, because things are getting serious.

When she finished with the socks, she glanced at the dryer and noticed it had about ten minutes to go. She dropped her head on her arms and closed her eyes, *just for a moment,* she told herself.

When she awoke with a start, she recognized Ed's voice at the top of the stairs: "Kathy, are you okay? Kathy?"

Sleep weighted her eyes, and her arms and hands had grown tingly from the weight of her head on them. She straightened, swallowed her exclamation, and replied, "I'll be right up. I guess I dozed off. Let me empty the dryer again."

"Not tonight, Kathy," Ed roared. "You've had enough. Come to bed right this minute."

She stood with a start and had to rein in her temper with all her might. She was not a child to be ordered around. Who did Ed think would do this if she didn't? He certainly couldn't come down the steps and do it himself! Not that she wanted him to, but why did he make it seem like some sort of crime for her to do it? Didn't he understand she only had a limited amount of time to get all the household chores done, and if she failed to make all her rounds they just piled deeper for when she could get to them? Why couldn't he understand?

"I'm coming in a minute," she called, well aware Ed would be angrier than ever by the time she got back upstairs.

The rest of the week went equally as poorly with Kathy barely dragging herself through the evenings. Ed became more and more disgruntled with her, and she became more and more tired. She knew something had to give, but what?

The following Friday night Ed insisted he needed charge of the alarm clock. "You are not getting up early tomorrow," he'd told her, and he took the clock and crammed it into a drawer across the room.

Kathy was too tired to protest. She didn't have to go to any of her jobs. She just needed to finish the never-ending pile of laundry, and there were meals to prepare and freeze for the coming week so Ed and Desmond would have something to eat while she went to her evening job. Someday soon she needed to wash the windows, because fall was coming and before long it would be too cold to tackle such a huge job.

All those jobs loomed on the horizon, and she'd been foolish enough to volunteer to help decorate some of the classrooms at church the next day. Weekends were, theoretically, free days for Kathy, but in actual fact she seldom took time to do anything she wanted to do or could enjoy. Decorating the classrooms was one of her special talents and she couldn't bring herself to give up the job, since each quarter several of the teachers depended on her for ideas and ways to carry them out.

Margaret, the preacher's wife, would be there with Quinthia, their adopted four-year-old daughter. She and Desmond always had fun playing at their mothers' feet, and that added to Kathy's enjoyment of the project.

The problem was, she didn't see any way to sleep late and then steal enough time to go to the church and help for very long at all. She needed to get up at her usual time, and tonight she just didn't have the strength to argue. Ed had already rolled his wheelchair to Desmond's bed and settled him for the night. Times like tonight Kathy was thankful they had had the sense to lower Desmond's crib so Ed could work his son in and out of it from his wheelchair. Although it was rather low for Kathy, it seemed that more and more the bedtime routine had fallen to Ed's care. He insisted it was at least one thing he could do, and he enjoyed the time with Desmond. They were becoming "buddies."

It did thrill Kathy to see the two of them play and giggle each evening, or to watch her son sit and point at the bright pictures in one of his books as Ed read to him. Only now and then did she feel a pang of jealousy at not having the time to do those things herself.

She kept reminding herself she had Desmond in the car to and from daycare every day, and they sang and babbled all the way. She reconciled herself with those thoughts, but sometimes it just wasn't enough. It wasn't giving her son her undivided attention. She had to share him with her driving and the attention she gave to the traffic, road signs, weather conditions, and myriad other interferences. Tonight she didn't want to think about those things. She just wanted to sleep. Maybe tomorrow would be a different day, and Scripture said, "Sufficient unto the day is the evil thereof." She knew that meant she shouldn't worry about tomorrow, for it would bring enough trouble without her adding more.

She dropped into bed where her back and limbs ached and sleep eluded her. She tried to will her mind and body to relax. She knew some self-hypnosis exercises to bring on the relaxation she so deeply craved, but each time she tried to concentrate on willing her legs to relax, her mind revolted and thoughts of the job at the investment company intruded into the serene scene she tried to produce.

She fought them off and started again. Her feet quit aching so badly and she sighed and willed the relaxation to advance up her legs.

What if the manager from Frosty Freeze Ice Cream & Sandwich Shoppe called tomorrow while she was decorating Sunday school rooms? They had been having trouble with one of the deep fryers and Kathy seemed to be the only one who could coax it to fry up another day's worth of French fries. If she were not at home, her supervisor would not know where to find her.

She forced the thoughts from her mind. The place had run before she hired on, and they could cope now. Nobody was indispensable, in spite of what she thought. Someone would get the fryer to work, or they would order a new one. She could not be on 24-hour call, and she did not want to be depended on so intently.

She started once again with her now stiffened feet. Perhaps she would do better with prayer than with self-hypnosis.

Lord, she began, *you know our needs, and I'm too tired to worry about them anymore. Help us to find ways to cope with all this, and help us to recognize the help when you send it. This is all yours now.*

She knew from experience that sleep would claim her in an instant. She also knew when she awoke, unless God really did step in, the problems would all be right there to greet her.

Chapter 4

Kathy awoke the next morning more refreshed than she had been in weeks. When she glanced at the clock she squealed, "Ed, you let me sleep way too late. I'll never make it to the church by nine o'clock!"

Ed wheeled to the bedroom door, already dressed and holding Desmond on his lap. "I called Margaret and told her you might be a little late."

Kathy fished beneath the edge of the bed for her house slippers, then dashed to the kitchen to pour a quick cup of coffee. "You should have called me. I hate being late."

She took the coffee back to the bathroom and washed her face and dried it before going to the closet to pull out a clean sweater and slacks. She dressed quickly, smoothed on a bit of makeup, gulped the last of her coffee, and headed for Desmond's room.

"You can't go without at least a little breakfast," Ed protested.

"I don't have time," she insisted as she checked Desmond's diaper bag to be sure it was well supplied. As she stuffed an extra handful of diapers inside, she carried the bag to the kitchen to grab a couple of sippy cups.

Ed sat at the table spooning cereal into Desmond as fast as the baby could consume it. "Desmond isn't finished yet. You might as well sit down and have a bite."

Kathy glanced at the two of them and saw a good bit of cereal remained in Desmond's bowl. It would be another five minutes before her son would be finished, and she couldn't deprive him of his meal. She could do without, but she would never make her son do so. She pulled a box of toasted oats from the cabinet and shook a helping into a bowl. That wouldn't take long to eat, and she would feel better with something in her stomach.

As soon as the baby finished, Kathy rose and poured the remainder of her dish into the disposal and reached for Desmond. "I have to go, Ed. Do you have everything you need?"

"I'll be just fine," he assured her as he wheeled to the door. "Go on, and enjoy your day."

Kathy strapped Desmond into the car seat and drove as quickly as she could. A speeding ticket would only slow her more, and besides, she'd taken to heart all the Scripture. Often it was a struggle to keep her foot light on the accelerator. She tried harder now than she used to before she read about how God expected his people to be law-abiding citizens.

She glanced at her watch just as she parked in the church lot. Margaret would already have all the supplies spread out, ready for Kathy to apply her expertise to arranging them.

Desmond babbled, giggled, and patted Kathy's face when she lifted him from his seat. She sucked in a quick breath of gratitude for this small replica of Ed. What would she do without her two men? She'd almost lost Ed last summer when that hothead shot him. She still remembered how frightened she'd been. If it hadn't been for Micah and Margaret and all their church family, she was sure she would have lost her faith and all purpose for even continuing to try to meet the many challenges that incident had instigated.

She shook her head, picked up Desmond, and started inside. Now was not the time she wanted to dwell on her problems. She and Ed were blessed to have him still alive, working any job at all, let alone the good one he now held. They had so many things to be thankful for. Money problems seemed to always magnify everything, but Kathy knew God would provide a way for them to cope. She wasn't sure how, but she knew he would. She and Ed just needed to give God time to work that plan.

When Kathy reached the teachers' supply room, Margaret stood in the midst of a circle of posters and large plastic packets of various bulletin board borders and decorations. Kathy marveled at this middle-aged woman who had been so good to her and her family. Even dressed in casual slacks and sweater, Margaret looked like she belonged on a magazine cover. Kathy couldn't fathom how the woman kept herself so perfectly groomed, especially now that she and Micah had adopted a little girl. Everyone knew kids destroyed your fashion persona; that was, everyone except Margaret. She always seemed to know exactly what to wear to compliment her curly brown hair and her petite figure. Kathy could only wish for such fashion savvy.

"Oh, hi, Kathy," Margaret said. "I was just trying to decide what we need. I'm glad you're here. You know how helpless I am with this sort of thing."

Kathy chuckled and asked, "Where's Quinthia?"

Margaret nodded toward the classroom next door. "Over there. She has an improvised tent all set up for herself and Desmond. There's a pallet and everything."

"Great. I'll be right back." Kathy strolled into the classroom where Quinthia waited. "Hi, sweetheart. How are you this morning?"

The dark-haired, olive-skinned little girl Micah and Margaret had adopted only a few months ago sat on the pallet and said, "I'm fine, thank you. I'm waiting for Desmond." Her dark eyes glittered with anticipation.

Kathy stared a moment at the perfect manners. Micah and Margaret had worked on that with this little girl, and it was beginning to show. Kathy stooped and plunked Desmond beside Quinthia. "Well, here he is, kiddo. Be gentle with him, okay?"

Quinthia nodded and, in a serious four-year-old tone, said, "Oh, I'm always careful with Desmond. He's my friend."

Kathy knew it was true, or she would never think of leaving Desmond in a room away from her. As it was, she would be just outside the door working in the hallway, and would be able to see and hear the children as they played. "He has some toys in the diaper bag," she told Quinthia, who promptly began to rummage to see what goodies were buried deep inside the bag.

Kathy went back to Margaret. "You do have a sense of color and balance, in spite of what you say. Your taste is impeccable."

"Maybe in home decorating," Margaret agreed. "I didn't grow up in church, and I have no clue what the kids will or won't like."

"You seem to know what pleases Quinthia," Kathy countered as she rummaged through the bags of borders.

"I do okay at home, and with clothes and that sort of thing, but this Bible class stuff is all new to me." Margaret moved a couple of stacks of posters nearer.

"Well, let's see the teacher's manual." Kathy flipped to the index of the leaflet. "We might want to use a story theme for this first part of the quarter, or we could use a seasonal theme."

The women worked together for an hour or more, taking only short breaks to help keep the children entertained and within sight and sound. They had almost finished when Kathy decided it was now or never. She had to talk to someone or she would surely break into thousands of pieces before long. She turned to Margaret. "Can I talk to you about something serious?"

Margaret seemed to sense exactly how important this was for Kathy, because she laid her work aside. "Of course. Do you want to sit down?"

Kathy hadn't considered that. Now that Margaret mentioned it, the idea sounded most attractive. "That would be good. Think the kids will be okay if we sit across the hall?"

"It's only another step or two away. We can still see and hear them," Margaret assured as she led Kathy to a seat, then waited for her to speak.

The trouble was, Kathy wasn't sure where to start. Did she start with the shooting? Margaret already knew all about that. She'd been there when it happened, and she'd been there all during the long hard recovery, just as Micah had. Kathy couldn't tell Margaret anything she didn't already know about all that. She also knew about the generous gifts of money the church members had given Ed the day he returned from the hospital. How did she say what was troubling her without sounding petulant and petty?

Margaret waited silently, but it was a comfortable silence. Kathy knew that what this newly converted preacher's wife lacked in experience she made up in love. Margaret loved all people, and it simply bubbled up unbidden for everyone. She held a special love for Kathy and her family, and Kathy could feel it every time she was around this kind woman.

Still, it was hard to get the words past her lips. Finally she sighed, squared her shoulders and admitted, "I'm struggling with my faith, Margaret. I know Scripture says God will take care of us, and at least intellectually I believe that. I have to admit, though, on a gut level I'm beginning to doubt." Kathy grabbed a tissue and mopped at her eyes, because the wretched things betrayed her turmoil by leaking huge tears onto her cheeks.

Margaret leaned over and opened her arms. "Come here."

She didn't have to ask twice. Kathy flung herself into Margaret's embrace and let her sobs escape in a mad rush. "I don't—I don't know— what we're—going to do." She wailed. "Ed is—working everyday—for Bruce— and he gets paid well—but . . ."

Kathy blubbered on, feeling like a small child rather than the responsible adult she was supposed to be. "I have two jobs . . . and the pay is good . . . at least for the day job . . . and even at Frosty Freeze I make more than most of the help. I should be thankful . . . not whining like this."

Margaret didn't reply. She just held Kathy and let her talk.

Kathy felt the warmth of her love and drew strength from it, so she continued: "We would be on top of the world . . . if only . . ." She stopped and bit her lip. She couldn't stop the rush of words any more than she could calm a tornado. "Margaret, why did God let that man shoot Ed? If Ed could walk and we didn't have all those medical bills, we would be fine." She rushed to amend herself. "We would be more than fine. Everything would be wonderful."

Margaret rocked her a bit back and forth, as she would Quinthia. "I know, Kathy. I've wondered about it myself, and I don't know why. I've asked Micah, too, and he can't answer, except to say we're not promised we won't suffer in this world. In fact, Scripture says we *will* suffer. That suffering takes different forms for different people. In the end, if we endure we almost always come out stronger. Maybe God is strengthening you and Ed, or someone who knows you."

"But what if we don't endure," Kathy sobbed. "What if we break?"

"You won't. You've been through too much already for you to break now." Margaret pushed Kathy back so their gazes could meet, and Kathy dropped her gaze, unable to look at Margaret's inquiring eyes.

"Kathy, what's hurting you most right now?"

Kathy paused, trying to form the words of her shame. How could she complain after God had been so good to spare Ed's life? Hadn't Bruce offered Ed a job and tricked him into learning the skills he needed to do it? Yet, did he do all that just to let them drown in financial ruin? Kathy swallowed back her anger.

"We can't pay all our bills. The hospital has been good to wait until the insurance paid all their portion, but now they want the rest, and we don't have enough left after the other bills to do more than a few dollars a month. They aren't satisfied with that, and we can't do any more. I don't know what we're going to do. I'm so tired I can barely function, and Ed can't get transportation for another job, even if there were something more he could do. The city is even talking about cutting what bus service he has now. I don't have any idea how he'll get to work if that happens."

Margaret squeezed Kathy's arms in gentle assurance. "Kathy, you're carrying a much heavier load than most women can imagine, but God will provide. Have you prayed about all this?"

"Oh, yeah," Kathy said. "I can't seem to do much of anything else about it, so I pray a lot."

Margaret nodded, then said, "But you obviously haven't turned it over to God. If you had, you would be calmer than this. Micah says that when you give something to God in prayer, you aren't supposed to pick it up and carry it out of the room when you leave."

Kathy sobbed harder: "But, that is exactly what I don't know how to do. I don't know how to give all this to God. He isn't going to magically plop all that money into our bank account. Scripture says somewhere that God helps those who help themselves."

Margaret smiled. "I don't think that is exactly what it says. You're right that we have to do our part. Aren't you doing that? Don't you go to work—even two jobs? Don't you manage your money well, without any waste that I can see?"

"Yes," Kathy nodded. "But I don't see any improvement. The bills are still there, and we still can't pay them all."

Margaret sat silent so long Kathy thought she must be as stymied as herself. When Margaret did speak it was with firm determination.

"Okay, here's the plan. With your permission, I'll talk to Micah about all this, and in the meantime we can both pray about it. And I'll ask Lacey to pray, too."

Kathy nodded. Micah had a new secretary and Kathy liked the nice single woman who seemed so efficient at her job. When Micah hired her, Margaret had explained that Micah normally preferred an older secretary. He'd been impressed because Lacey had been very nice and so efficient, and she was a fairly new Christian herself. She'd been baptized in the East where she'd lived with her parents. Both had been killed in a plane crash on the way to a business meeting in Japan. Lacey needed a job desperately, and Micah needed a secretary. With Margaret's full approval, the arrangement was made to the advantage of both.

Kathy liked Lacey a lot. She was efficient, and she went out of her way to help the members with their needs. She had such a caring attitude, people couldn't help but like her.

"Good," Margaret said when Kathy blew her nose. "Now, let's go find Lacey and say our first prayer right now."

Chapter 5

Kathy had barely cleared the drive when Ed switched on his computer. He intended to go over the accounting program and see exactly where their money had gone the past couple of months. Surely there was something they could economize on until they got his hospital and therapy bills under control.

It didn't take long for him to determine again that Kathy had already trimmed the budget to the bare bones. She didn't even buy disposable diapers for Desmond anymore except to take to daycare. That meant a lot of extra work for her, but she insisted it was cheaper for her to launder cloth diapers, and apparently it was. Ed had volunteered to fold Desmond's clothes when she first suggested the idea, and he now finished almost all the laundry when she bothered to bring it up from the basement. As often as not she folded it herself, saying she was waiting for the next load to cycle anyway, so she might as well do it while she was there.

Ed supposed that made sense, but he hated to see Kathy so worn down, so tired all the time. He wanted to do everything he could to make her days and evenings easier. There wasn't much he could do, except folding laundry, which was one thing he could manage quite well, if she would just let him.

Ed closed the financial program and clicked on the Internet icon. He might as well play a game or two online since there was nowhere to go. The buses didn't run on Saturday, and LaMont had said he was busy this morning. Ed didn't know anyone else with a vehicle big enough to accommodate him and his wheelchair, or who had the strength to hoist it around. He would be stuck here until Kathy came home.

He found a game he usually enjoyed, however it held little pleasure for him today. He went to Google, his favorite search engine, and keyed in "poker," just to see if there were other people who enjoyed a friendly online game. The results of the search staggered him. There were hundreds of sites, and as he scanned through, he could see there were many for real, serious gambling, not just the friendly game he had in mind. He clicked on a few links, telling himself he just wanted to see what they were all about. His curiosity built. He wondered how money transfers worked over the net.

As he surfed, it became clear the games were for real cash, and some sites even offered a substantial stake to start the player off. *What could it hurt to just play with their free offer? I'm not using any of my money. It might be fun to see how I stack up with the big boys.*

Google revealed many URLs that offered free poker games. Ed decided to try it. Free couldn't hurt anyone, and if the computer was rigged, he could lose without anyone getting hurt. If he won, he would know it was possible. Kathy would be gone until well after lunch, so he had time to explore as much as he wanted.

He chastised himself for wanting to hide this innocuous game from Kathy. He wasn't hurting anyone. It was only a game. He merely wanted to see if he *could* beat the computer, or the other online players. It wasn't like he was playing for real money. Still, he knew it would upset his wife, and she had enough on her mind the way it was.

He clicked onto one of the free sites and logged in. This particular game was wagered in points. In moments he sat deeply engrossed in each hand. Even though he lost the first, he knew that often happened. The proof of the game was playing many hands. That's when you earned big money.

The second hand he won. It wasn't much, only twenty-five points, but it proved to him that it was possible to win in this setting. He played another hand.

The next time he glanced at the clock, it read eleven-thirty, and Ed held five hundred points on his screen. He grinned. He still had his touch. He was still King of Aces!

Kathy would be home soon, so he needed to get off the computer.

Ed knew he was venturing into a dangerous arena, but if he could just win some real money—not if, but when he won—maybe he could pay some of those bills that were stacked right here beneath his hands.

He had to get Kathy some relief, and soon. Ed knew Kathy loved him, but even she could break under all this stress. He was no longer the man she'd married, and she hadn't signed up for a lifetime with a cripple who couldn't even pay all his own bills. It plagued him constantly, wondering just how long Kathy would be able to endure this new lifestyle. When would she decide she'd had enough and leave for greener pastures?

Ed didn't want to think such thoughts, but he didn't seem able to completely banish them from his brain. Kathy loved him. He knew she was also human, and at times he knew he wanted to run away from all this. If he wanted to, what must Kathy be feeling?

As much as the thought of losing her terrified him, he knew he couldn't blame her if she did get enough and leave him someday.

Each time those thoughts reared their ugly heads, he reassured himself that even if Kathy felt tempted to leave, she was committed to God, and she would honor her wedding vows. Even that assurance rang hollow, because he didn't want her to stay just because of a sense of duty. Besides, even if she chose not to get a divorce, it didn't mean she had to stay and live with him.

Ed forced those thoughts from his mind. He had enough problems without all this. He needed to play a game or two and quit all this morbid hashing of what might happen. Since he couldn't do anything to help the situation at the moment, he might as well divert himself with a game.

He decided to do an extensive search to find the sights that offered the largest free stakes. If things went well, over time he might even want to play on more than one site with those free enticements.

As he searched out the best games, he wrote each URL in a notebook. He didn't want to bookmark them in case Kathy should use the computer and ask about them. It bothered him to know she would not approve of what he was doing, but he had to do something to help her, and this was one way he could.

He felt sure he could beat the odds. After all, he didn't earn the title of King of Aces by losing. He'd won time and again against LaMont and all his friends, and anyone else who came along. He'd won this morning online. All he needed now was a chance to play for real stakes. He could feel the relief inside already. It would be so good to see Kathy relaxed and not having to work two jobs. If he could just play enough to get them out of debt, then he would quit.

Kathy came home around one in the afternoon, and by that time Ed had hidden away his notebook and the computer sat idle.

"How was your morning?" she asked as she plunked Desmond onto his daddy's lap and set her purse on a nearby chair. She took the sippy cups from Desmond's diaper bag and put them in the kitchen sink.

Ed knew she could still hear him when she returned and headed to Desmond's room with the bag. "The same," he said. "Just played some games on the computer. Not much else I can do around here."

Kathy returned and dropped onto the old brown sofa. "I know, Ed. I wish we had a specially equipped car so you could get out more, and I wish there was more money, but we are so blessed to be as well-off as we are."

Ed gritted his teeth, knowing in his head that Kathy was right, but in his heart anger bubbled in a slow simmer. Kathy deserved more, much more than they had or hoped to have anytime soon. Thanks to his activity this morning, he knew a way to lighten that load, and he intended to do it, just as soon as he could manage some more time alone.

Chapter 6

Ed didn't have to wait long for his opportunity. Kathy had to go to her Frosty Freeze job that evening, so Ed placed Desmond in the playpen at one side of the living room and added a stack of toys in one corner. He knew Desmond would be quite content until he needed something to eat or a diaper change. Desmond wasn't like a lot of babies who fussed all the time. If there were plenty of toys, he preferred to be left to his own devices, rather than being held or handed from person to person to be entertained. Ed's gratitude swelled again when he thought about Desmond and how little he demanded of his parents as compared to other babies.

Ed rolled to the desk and clicked on the computer. In mere moments he had keyed in the URL of what he felt would be the best site that offered practice rounds. The old rush whipped through him, and soon he was deep into play.

The rounds played out quickly, and before he knew it he had played over ten hands, and using the original free stakes, he'd multiplied his money by five. This practice didn't actually win or lose money. If he could win here, he was sure he would be able to win in the real games. He had wanted to see if the machine was fair. It surprised and pleased him when he won more hands than he lost. He didn't try to suppress his broad grin. Nobody could see him. He could practice his poker face at other times. Here he didn't have to hide his pleasure. He was alone, except for Desmond, and the baby certainly didn't know what was happening.

Ed enjoyed a winning streak, so he decided to continue to play. He had nothing else to do, and he told himself he could always quit if he lost. He wasn't losing, and the more experience he got, the better off he and Kathy would be.

Hand after hand, Ed played, occasionally losing a round. That was to be expected. Running the averages, he was well ahead of his beginning stake.

He could do this for real, and soon.

Something niggled at the back of his mind telling him nobody beat the odds all the time. He knew that. To his delight he'd just proved he could win more hands than he lost. It was a matter of knowing what to do with the cards that were dealt. He was good at that, and he knew the strategy to win. All he had to do was keep his mind on the game, and he couldn't be stopped.

He pushed down the argument that if someone won it meant someone else lost. He dismissed all such thoughts promptly. The casinos could afford to lose occasionally. With no remorse, they took money from the smucks who didn't know how to win. He knew he wouldn't win all the time, and the casinos would spare no mercy on him when he lost. He didn't need to feel guilty about taking money from them when he won.

Ed knew how to control his losses. When he began to lose, he needed to quit for a session or two and revitalize his concentration. He didn't have time to gamble all the time anyway, and all he wanted was enough money to help Kathy quit work. He didn't want or expect to get rich. He just wanted some relief from their day-to-day bills. He wanted to feel like a man again.

Who could object if he won enough money to get that ease of mind?

Desmond started to fuss, so Ed turned from the computer and took his son into his arms. He rolled the two of them to the kitchen and poured a sippy cup full of apple juice for his son. As soon as Desmond finished, Ed took him to the living room and changed his diaper.

Crankiness clung to the boy, so Ed picked him up and, using their hands, helped Desmond do several squat and stand exercises on his daddy's lap. The baby giggled and squealed, and Ed laughed with him as he sang a silly nursery rhyme.

Soon both grew tired, and Ed stuffed wiggly arms and legs into the warm pajamas Kathy had laid out, then put Desmond to bed. Ed glanced at the clock. Kathy would not be home for an hour and a half.

He rolled back to the computer and clicked it on. In moments he was on a real gambling site, not one of the practice sites. He'd chosen one with bonus stakes to start, aware the casinos expected that money to be lost promptly. Ed had no such intention. He studied the instructions on how to start, and then went to where it told how to deposit his gambling stakes. It amazed him at the variety of ways money could be placed into an online gambling account. The screen indicated it only took two to three minutes for the money to be credited. He could start playing right away.

The deposit limit with a credit card was twenty dollars. That was good. He could afford twenty dollars, because if he should lose, he could do without lunches for a few days and still be okay. Since he paid the bills, Kathy would have no reason to know he'd made this deposit, and with the bonus stake the casino offered, he would have a nice little pot to start. The small limit also reassured him that he wouldn't stumble into a high-stakes game and embarrass himself by having his tiny bets outranked before he even had a chance to win.

He glanced at the clock in the lower right corner of his computer to be sure it was correct. It wasn't, so he went into the control panel and updated it. He certainly didn't want Kathy to come home and find him on this site. He also didn't want to analyze why that felt so wrong. He just wanted to play—except for him it wasn't play any longer. Now, it was dead serious.

It took some time to download the software, register, and set up his account, and he wondered how he would keep it from Kathy if she should use his computer. He decided to worry about that later. He did take the precaution to delete the icon from the desktop. He would access the game from the directory. Right now he had work to do, and he knew it was indeed now work, not just a game.

His first game involved six players, and the stakes were higher than Ed had anticipated. Even so, he knew he could win. He felt it deep within himself.

He wasn't disappointed in the first few hands. He took the pot three hands in a row. On the fourth hand he lost, but he'd only bet a portion of his winnings. He was still ahead, and he'd known he wouldn't win every round. As long as he kept some of his winnings back each time, he would end up in the lead. His opposing players were good, too, so it took all his concentration to keep winning. He couldn't afford any stupid mistakes. He wouldn't. He'd played this game so much as a kid and in prison. Most of the plays came as second nature to him. He watched as his account climbed, and he was just getting in stride when he glanced at the clock in the corner of the computer. Kathy would be home soon. He had to sign off.

He knew he would be back. He had found what could be the solution to his and Kathy's problems, and he intended to utilize it, and the sooner the better.

Moments after he turned the computer off, Kathy opened the door, and carried a bag of groceries inside. She looked exhausted as usual.

"How was your evening?" he asked her when she came back from the kitchen and dropped into the overstuffed chair beside the door.

She flexed her shoulders, obviously trying to loosen the stiff muscles down her back. "It was okay. We were really busy. Football game got out about ten, and we had a rush. After that things got quiet. All we had to do was police the place, and that didn't take as long as usual. I am tired." She closed her eyes a moment. "I remembered we were almost out of milk, so I had to stop at the store."

Kathy's words pierced Ed's heart. He could see how tired Kathy was without her telling him. Truth be known, she appeared even more worn out than she said. She looked terrible.

"Some day you'll be able to stay home and not have to do that anymore," he promised.

Kathy sighed, "It's going to be a long time, I can tell you that right now. We have enough bills to keep us both working for a lot of years."

"Maybe not," Ed said. "Maybe I can do something to earn more money."

Kathy shook her head. "You're already doin' everything we know for you to do, and we can't both work evenings. Somebody has to watch Desmond, and besides, you wouldn't have transportation to an evening job. You're just blessed to have the cerebral palsy van come by and pick you up for your day job. No way they're going to drive you at night, too."

"I know," Ed agreed, "but maybe somethin' will come up. I'm thinkin' all the time. You never know."

"Well," Kathy said before she rose from her chair, "you go right on thinkin'. Right now I have to wash another load of diapers and get to bed."

Ed nodded. He knew he would find a time to get back online and start doing some serious money gathering. He would get Kathy out of that job just as soon as possible.

Before Kathy came back upstairs the phone rang.

Ed reached for it beside the computer. "Hello."

Ed recognized the preacher's voice immediately. Micah was a good friend and he knew their lifestyle, so it didn't alarm Ed that he'd called this late. Still something had to be amiss.

"Ed, Quinthia's temperature has spiked, and we're on our way to the hospital. I wondered if you would call LaMont tomorrow and tell him he'll have to come to the church a little later. He was going to start a window washing project in the morning before it got too hot. I won't be there with the key, and Lacey doesn't come in until after nine."

Ed thought a moment. His brother, LaMont, had taken over Ed's custodial job at the church when Ed was shot. LaMont still lived in the inner city with their mother. Ed knew both his mother and LaMont would be in bed by this time, as Micah seemed to know also. "I can call, Micah, but it shouldn't keep him from being able to do the outsides of the windows, should it? The ladders and brushes are in the garage."

"Right," Micah agreed. "Trouble is, the garage door opener is in the office. He'll have to wait. I'm sorry about this, but we can't afford to wait till morning with Quinthia."

"No, I know," Ed agreed. "We'll be praying for her, Micah, and you be careful. It's late."

"We'll be fine," Micah said over the line. "Mercy Hospital has good staff in the ER round the clock, but do pray, and I'll call you as soon as I know anything."

Kathy came upstairs and asked, "Who was that at this hour?"

"Micah," Ed said. "They're taking Quinthia back to the hospital. Her temperature's spiking."

"Oh no!" Kathy sank onto the chair again. "Do they think it's her leukemia, or maybe it's just a bad cold or something?"

"He didn't say, but he sounded worried." Ed hated to tell Kathy such bad news this late at night. She would lie awake worrying and praying, and tomorrow she would be even more exhausted.

He had to get serious about winning them some relief soon.

Chapter 7

It took Kathy more time than she had planned to get Desmond dressed, fed, and to the daycare center before she'd finally made it to work. She took a few minutes to orient herself to the day's schedule, took care of all the pressing issues, and then picked up the phone.

She dialed Mercy Hospital from memory. Margaret and Micah had already spent a lot of time there with their adopted daughter, Quinthia, when she was being treated for leukemia. The child's illness had been in remission for quite some time now. Unfortunately, they never knew when it would flare again. It was like living on the edge of an active volcano. You never knew when it would erupt and destroy your life.

"Is there a Quinthia Forrest registered?" she asked the information operator. "It's spelled Q-u-i-n-t-h-i-a."

The seconds it took the woman to check her computer seemed to be eons. "She's in room 695. Would you like me to transfer your call?"

"Yes, please," Kathy said, and waited until Margaret lifted the phone.

Kathy didn't bother with pleasantries. "Margaret, what's going on? I've been so worried."

"Quinthia is running a rather high temperature, and we didn't want to take any chances. The doctors still aren't sure what it is. They've put us in isolation. They think it may be as simple as a childhood disease, but we don't know for sure. Chickenpox is going around the city right now, and they suspect that may be the culprit."

Kathy dismissed that possibility flat out. "Hasn't she had her shots? I would think getting all her vaccinations would have been a priority with her history."

"Of course," Margaret assured her. "I guess sometimes the kids can get a mild case even when they've been vaccinated. Actually, I doubt that's what's going on here, but they're looking at all the possibilities. I suspect it's just some sort of virus."

Kathy sagged onto a chair. "Oh, I certainly hope so. She's come so far with the leukemia, I sure don't want to see her relapse now."

"None of us do, Kathy. Just remember God is in control, and there's a new doctor here who really knows about leukemia. Even if it is a flareup, he's confident they can treat it quickly and put her back in remission. He says there are different kinds of leukemia, and they've had some great results with what Quinthia has."

Kathy bit her lower lip. She knew Margaret was right when she said God was in control. It was just that sometimes it was awfully hard to believe it deep inside. It was one thing to know a thing in your head and another to accept it in your heart.

Kathy and Ed had experienced so many of God's blessings from Micah and Margaret, and from Bruce. Kathy remembered all those things. Still, she wondered why God had quit now. He gave them all those blessings only to later make them suffer what seemed to her to be insurmountable struggles. She pushed those negative thoughts down deep into her inner self. She didn't want to look at them. She didn't want to hurt any longer. She didn't want to know why God had deserted them after all they had already gone through. She was just thankful God seemed to still be favoring Quinthia.

"They don't think it is a relapse?"

"Not yet anyway. It will be a few hours before we know anything. In the meantime, pray. Okay?" Margaret's voice sounded strong and not especially worried. She probably just wanted to cover all the bases, including prayer.

"You know I will," Kathy promised. "Is there anything I can do to help while you're stuck there?"

Margaret hesitated a moment, then said, "If you're sure you have time, it would help me a lot if you would teach the ladies' class this evening. I know you always have your lesson prepared ahead, and we usually just read the Scriptures and the questions in the book and discuss them. It shouldn't be too hard."

Kathy smiled. "I can do that. I taught several times before you met Micah and started coming. We'll be fine."

"I know you will," Margaret agreed, "or I wouldn't have asked. And thanks, Kathy."

Kathy hung up and gathered some of the papers on her desk, intent on reducing the mound resting there.

Over an hour later she thought about the class again. Lacey would attend, and Kathy knew she would be willing to read some of the Scriptures. Some of the women wouldn't, begging off for one reason or another, but Lacey was always available.

Immediately behind that thought came the idea that they needed to invite Lacey's aunt, Zoe Brenner.

Kathy dialed the church. "Lacey, I talked to Margaret a little bit ago, and she asked me to teach the ladies' class tonight. I just wondered if you thought it would help if I called your Aunt Zoe to invite her. I know you said she wouldn't come when you asked her."

Lacey's voice sounded pensive. "I don't know. It just might work. She's funny. One time she's totally not interested, and the next time she's all for coming. I never know what to expect."

Kathy picked up a pen. "Give me her number, and I'll call. The worst thing she can do is say no. If she agrees, we're one step closer to our goal."

Lacey gave Kathy the number, and then added, "You might pray before you call. Aunt Zoe is a nice woman, and she's fun, and she has good morals, but she sees no reason to need religion. She's sort of stubborn, too."

Kathy laughed. "I know a few other people with that trait. It can be a problem, but used right, that same stubborn trait has caused some great things to be done in the past."

"Yes, I know," Lacey replied, "like all the inventors who refused to give up, and people who founded organizations against all odds. I would love to see Aunt Zoe channel her stubborn streak like that. Problem is, right now the only manifestation I see is her refusing to come to church with me."

"Yes, but just think what a force she'll be when you do win her over."

Lacey giggled on the other end of the phone line. "I haven't given up hope, but I'm not holding my breath, either."

"I'll give her a call," Kathy said, before she hung up.

It surprised her somewhat when Zoe sounded delighted to hear from her.

"Well, Kathy, what a nice surprise. I'd love to go with you. Are you bringing that delightful baby with you?"

Kathy smiled. Zoe had taken an almost grandmotherly interest in Desmond, and if that was what it would take to get her to church, Kathy wasn't above using it. She wanted Zoe to come long enough to learn the gospel. "Not this time, Zoe. The usual sitter is ill, and I'll be teaching, so Ed is keeping Desmond. The sitter will be there next week," she hurried to add.

"Then maybe I'll wait 'til then to come," Zoe said.

"But you'll miss my teaching," Kathy said. "Margaret will be back by then, I'm sure. I'd really like for you to come tonight, and next week, too."

"Well," Zoe paused long enough to make Kathy think she would refuse before she heard Zoe go on, "I suppose I could come tonight. I was going to clean the refrigerator, but actually that doesn't sound like much fun."

"Good," Kathy said, "that's settled. I'll come by and pick you up, if you want me to."

"No need," Zoe said. "I can drive, or I may call Lacey and have her come to dinner. She's asked me to teach her how to make my special lasagna."

"Oh, yum," Kathy said. "That sounds heavenly. I'll see you tonight."

Guilt niggled at Kathy for leaving Ed alone to sit with Desmond so much, but she knew they would find something to do.

Chapter 8

That evening Ed played with Desmond for a bit, then put the baby in the playpen. Soon, however, he turned on his computer. He had work to do.

When the phone rang, it startled him, but not as much as the voice on the other end.

"Hey, Ed, it's LaMont! I'm at college, and you should see the athletic department here! Man, it is so cool! They have every piece of equipment imaginable."

Ed chuckled at his brother's enthusiasm. "You like it, huh?"

"Like it? Man, I ain't never seen so much stuff." Ed hadn't heard such excitement in LaMont's voice since the night he and all his basketball team mates won college scholarships. That euphoria had been robbed from LaMont the day Ed had been shot. None of the family had experienced much joy since then. It did Ed's heart good to hear LaMont so happy now. He could only hope and pray it would last. It was time for them all to get on with their lives and find a little fun now and then.

"So, tell me all about it, man." Ed wanted to share LaMont's excitement, and he wanted all the details.

"Like I said, there's all kinds of workout equipment, and we have practice every day. The coach drives us hard, and the guys on the basketball team are good. I'm good, too, but I'm gonna have to work to keep up with some of these guys. They're awesome!"

Ed chuckled. "What's the matter, little bro, you think you're not good enough any more?"

LaMont's voice sharpened. "No way, man. I'm good enough, but they keep gettin' better, so I have to work harder, too."

"Sounds right to me," Ed replied. "You've never been a stranger to work. You gonna be able to keep up at school and keep the job at church, too? Don't forget you need that money for books and stuff."

"I know. Micah says I can work early mornings and late nights. He gave me a key after that delay with the window washing. He'd planned to be in the office any time I was there, but he changed his mind after he and Margaret had to make that run to the hospital the other night."

Ed frowned at the reminder of Quinthia's illness. "Have you heard how that turned out? We've been praying for Quinthia for a long time."

"Micah says it looks like a cold. They ran some blood tests, and those aren't back yet, but the doctors are sending her home."

"Good," Ed snapped. "That little girl's been sick long enough. Did you get the windows done?"

"Most of them. I have the key so I can choose my times."

Ed leaned back in his chair and gripped the phone loosely. "It will be easier on you to be able to come and go whenever you want. Just don't forget to handle it like a man."

LaMont agreed. "It's best if other people aren't there when I do a lot of that stuff anyway."

Ed edged his chair closer to the desk. "Oh yeah, especially things like changing light bulbs in that high auditorium. I was always afraid someone would come along and knock my ladder over. Just don't forget to relock all the doors when you leave. You can't afford to pay for stuff that walks off—not that anyone there would expect you to, but our family honor would expect it, so just be careful, okay?"

LaMont laughed. "I'm older now, Bro, and I am also a little more responsible."

Ed couldn't help remembering all the lights he'd turned off, bikes and balls he'd stashed in storage, and doors he'd locked behind LaMont when he was younger, back when Ed had been a whole man. He knew LaMont was older now. Was he really more responsible? He certainly hoped so, especially since LaMont took the custodial job. If LaMont messed up, it would be a direct reflection on Ed.

"Just keep your mind on the job while you're there. That's all I'm saying," Ed replied.

LaMont switched the conversation to basketball and soon hung up.

Ed grinned as he turned back to his computer. His little brother was growing up, and with the scholarship Micah had helped the guys earn,

LaMont had a much brighter future than Ed had been able to anticipate at his age.

Ed sat and reflected for a few moments about how different things would have been if Micah hadn't come to the prison to teach him about God. Ed would probably never have made parole, he wouldn't have been able to marry Kathy, and LaMont would never have been on that inner-city basketball team. Because Micah was able to forgive and reach out to teach, not only did Ed, Kathy, and LaMont become Christians, but so did most of the guys on LaMont's team. Ed still struggled to understand it all.

He shook his head and turned on the computer. He appreciated all Micah had done for him and his family. Now he needed to do some things for himself. Micah couldn't help Ed out of his present financial crisis, and Ed realized it *was* a crisis. Up to now he'd felt certain something would come up, some miracle materialize, and things would all work out. That had not happened. Kathy grew wearier by the day. Ed couldn't see how she could go on much longer. When would she get enough and pack her bags and take Desmond to go live with her mom in California? Ed closed his eyes, determined to shut out that horrible thought. He had to get Kathy some relief—and soon.

It was obviously up to Ed to deal with this mess, and he knew how. All he had to do was win a few good hands of poker and things would be better.

He turned on the computer and keyed in the URL for the casino. In seconds he was deep into the game. The adrenaline flowed, he focused, and promptly lost the first hand.

No matter. Everyone lost a hand now and then. You just had to keep going and concentrate harder.

Ed waited for the second hand to be dealt. Desmond began to fuss, and Ed ignored him. It wouldn't hurt him to cry a few minutes.

Ed won the next hand, and he shouted with joy. His loud voice startled Desmond, who began to wail in earnest. Ed wheeled over and picked up his son and swiftly wheeled back to the computer. He held Desmond with one arm and clicked the mouse with the other, intent on winning another hand.

Desmond grew still and became engrossed in the rapid movement of the cards on the screen.

Ed played hand after hand, the adrenaline flowing faster each time he won. Desmond patted the screen and cooed often, and he seemed quite content to sit on Ed's lap.

When Ed glanced at the clock in the corner of his screen, he realized Kathy would be home soon, so he quickly signed off and shut the computer down.

He still needed to dress Desmond for bed and get him down. He let a broad smile escape. Things looked brighter than they had in a very long time. Tomorrow Ed would log on and transfer his winnings to his bank account. He would be able to pay at least most of the pressing bills.

Things were looking good.

Chapter 9

*E*d could barely wait to get home the following evening. When the specially equipped bus dropped him off, he wheeled to the mailbox first.

Another handful of bills waited there, but today he grinned. As soon as Kathy brought Desmond home and went to her evening job, Ed would go online again. This time would be different. This time there was money in his account. He could transfer that stash to the bank, and he could write checks for most of these bills. He didn't need to gamble any more. He just needed to transfer his money.

The feeling of relief was indescribable. He wished he could tell Kathy. She would be so happy to be released from her load of worry. It was a real shame he couldn't give her that gift of peace. He knew Kathy wouldn't approve. There was no telling exactly how she would react, but it wouldn't be good.

He frowned. He definitely intended to pay the overdue utility bills. The issue was how he would explain that to Kathy. Even though he was the one who wrote the checks, she knew where the money went, and she knew when there wasn't enough to go around. He would have to tell her the power was not going to be shut off next week after all. How could he explain to her without raising suspicion?

He needed to think this through, and he hadn't had time to do that yet. He would work on it tonight, after he paid the utilities up to date. It felt so good to know they would no longer be three months behind, and despite the repeated warning he now held in his hand, the electricity would not be turned off next Monday.

Ed stopped just short of thanking God for this blessing. Oh, he did consider it a blessing. Deep inside he knew God did not approve of his gambling. He wasn't exactly sure why, and he couldn't remember any Scriptures that talked about it. He did know every preacher he'd ever heard talk about it agreed it was evil.

Ed didn't see how his being able to pay his debts could be considered evil. If it was, it didn't come from God. He decided not to think about it any more.

Instead, he waited until Kathy left for her evening job, and then he went to work. In less than half an hour he had transferred enough money to pay all the utility bills and he'd written the checks and addressed and stamped the envelopes. Tomorrow he would mail them all.

When he finished, he turned to Desmond and spent several minutes playing with his son. The little boy bounced and giggled as his daddy lifted him up and down. When they both tired, Ed dressed Desmond in his pajamas and read to him until the toddler nodded off to sleep.

Ed wheeled him to the baby bed, kissed him, and tucked him in. That done, he rolled back to the computer.

There had been one letter his winnings had not helped so far. He sighed when he lifted the page to read again.

> It is with great regret that we must inform you of the closing of the public transportation assistance program. We are aware of the vast need, however the funding for this program has ended. Consequently, our last run will be the last Friday of this month. We recommend you write your legislators . . .

Ed laid the letter on the desk top. Without the bus service, he would have no way to get to work. Kathy couldn't drive him, drop Desmond off, and get to her job on time. Even if they got up extra early to manage all that, there would never be enough time for Kathy to get them all home and go on to her evening job on time. Kathy would have no choice. She would have to go somewhere for help. What sort of man would allow his wife to be reduced to begging?

Ed pounded the desk. "Where are you, God?" He demanded. "You promised we wouldn't be given more temptation than we can handle. So what am I supposed to do about this? What's going to happen to us if I lose my job? We can't pay all the bills now."

Ed ran his hand across his kinky skullcap. He needed a car of his own. Frustration boiled up. Even if he had a car, he wouldn't be able to drive it. He needed legs that worked in order to drive, and his hung limp from the seat of his chair. There seemed to be no solution, and yet he had to find one. He had to be able to go to work.

He rolled to the kitchen and gathered the little free local paper, then spread the classified ads so he could examine them.

He found only a couple of ads for ride sharing, and they were on the opposite side of town. Even if he had found something nearby, he knew there would have to be room for his wheelchair in the car, and someone to help him in and out of it. Not many people would be willing to do that.

He wadded the paper into a tight ball and slammed it into the trash can.

He had three weeks to find an answer. Three weeks sounded like plenty of time to address most situations. Ed wasn't sure this one would be resolved in a lifetime.

He wheeled back to the computer. The only thing he knew to do was try to win as much money as he could as fast as possible. God would just have to look the other way because Ed didn't see any other solution. He would quit gambling just as soon as he got over this hurdle. In the meantime surely God didn't expect him to let his family go hungry or get evicted.

Even great winnings wouldn't solve the problem. He could only hope they would keep the wolves from the door long enough for him to think of something.

Kathy had just shut her computer down at work and started to leave when the phone rang.

"This is Kathy. May I help you?"

Margaret Forrest said, "Hi, Kathy. I just called to let you know I'm home with Quinthia. Her fever broke and she's fine. Not even any chickenpox!"

"That's wonderful!" Kathy exclaimed. "Ed told me. Did they decide what caused the fever in the first place?"

"Apparently some sort of virus. Thank goodness, she's fine now. In fact, she had lost her appetite. Now she wants to stop by the pancake house and have breakfast again."

"Again?" Kathy asked, before she shuffled a handful of papers into her out tray.

"Yes, again," Margaret said. "She ate a bowl of cereal and some fruit earlier. Now she wants eggs and pancakes!"

Kathy laughed. "So, go feed that girl! She apparently needs to renew her strength and is making up for lost time."

"I guess," Margaret agreed. "I just wanted you to know our prayers were answered, at least this time."

Kathy shifted the receiver to her other ear and reached for another stack of papers to process. "We've known that all along. God is there, even when he says no."

"Yes, but it's nice when he says yes, and he did this time."

"Then go feed that child, and I'll see you in church." Kathy's tone was as light as her spirits. It did feel good to have her faith in prayer reaffirmed.

Kathy hung up, headed to the daycare center and picked up Desmond, then drove home. On the way, she reflected on her call from Margaret. It was so easy for her to forget God was faithful and trust him with her problems, too, when she was so deep in financial worries. She knew God would take care of those. Sometimes it was just hard to trust him to do so. She needed to pray more and turn it all over to God. She resolved to do her best, and she knew that had to be a better effort than she had made so far.

The minute she walked into the house, she knew something was terribly wrong. Ed sat slumped in his chair, eyes glazed and his hands clasped in his lap.

He glanced up when she stepped close. "Hi, Honey."

He didn't offer to kiss her, or to take Desmond. It wasn't like Ed at all.

"What's wrong," she asked before she sat Desmond in his highchair and gave him a cracker.

Ed shrugged and handed her the letter from the Department of Transportation.

Kathy scanned the letter quickly, and then dropped onto the old brown sofa. "Well, they told us weeks ago this could happen. I really didn't believe the city would actually go this far."

She struggled to keep the tears at bay. One set of tears a day was all she allowed herself, and she'd already used today's allotment for Quinthia.

The reasoning sounded good, and she intended to follow through, but this was almost too much. The only thing that saved her was the knowledge of what her tears would do to Ed. Her dear husband already had enough to agonize him without her sniveling all over the place.

"What do you think Bruce would say if you asked permission to work from home?" she asked, knowing it was probably a hopeless cause.

"There isn't any way I can. There are five men on each team working on our current contract. We brainstorm constantly, building new programs as we go. It takes the whole team onsite to do the job. If I could have worked at home, Bruce would never have moved me downtown in the first place. He knew the bus service wasn't cheap."

Kathy moved to the tattered rocker and dropped her hands into her lap, trying to think of a solution. She was too tired to be very original. For the best of her efforts, there was not so much as a glimmer of an idea that presented itself.

She sucked in a deep breath and pulled herself to her full height. "We'll just have to pray harder."

Ed glared at her before he snapped, "We've already prayed, and look where it's gotten us. I'm tired of praying. We need to do something— I just don't know what it is I'm supposed to do."

"Me, neither." Kathy sighed, and then added, "We can't quit praying, Ed. God is our only real hope in all this. Surely you can see that."

Ed's glare softened. "I suppose, but we need to keep thinking, too."

"Of course we do," Kathy agreed. She rose and grabbed her purse. "I have to go to work. We'll keep thinking and praying. Something will work out. You'll see."

Ed leaned forward to kiss his wife goodbye. He knew that even if he should pray, God would never listen to his prayers while he was busy solving this problem in the only way he knew how.

Chapter 10

When Kathy left, Ed picked up the letter again and read it closely. Nothing changed. The bus service was still ending, so he slipped the page back into the envelope. When he did, he noticed a small flyer that had stuck inside.

He pulled it out and studied it. A local company was advertising various alterations to regular cars so handicapped persons could drive.

Ed's heart raced, his mouth went dry, and his hands shook. He didn't dare dream he might be able to utilize one of those cars. If by some miracle a car could be retrofitted to operate with just his hands, there would be no end to the things he could do. He would be able to take on many of the errands Kathy barely had time to manage. If they could find a sitter for Desmond, he could even look for an evening job, too.

The grin on Ed's face spread wide as he contemplated the freedom such a vehicle would represent. Of course, it would have to be a van with a lift so he could roll himself inside. Kathy already drove a van. If it could be retrofitted, they could buy a small inexpensive car for Kathy.

Ed had no idea how long it would take to learn to drive using only his hands. But he was certain he could do it.

He allowed his mind to race along, imagining all the places he could go, and the things he would be able to do.

It was several minutes before reality slammed into his chest. He couldn't pay the bills now. Where would he get the money for another car payment and insurance premiums, let alone gas, oil, tires, and regular maintenance? It was a nice dream to think of driving again. Too bad there was no way he could pay for that much-coveted freedom.

He crushed the brochure in his fist and slammed it into the trash can.

Ed dropped his head into his hands and shuddered a long sigh. What were he and Kathy supposed to do when the bus service ended? They would be homeless in a matter of weeks, and Ed could see no way to prevent it.

He sat there several minutes before Desmond's fussing jolted him out of his black haze.

"Sorry, Buddy," he said as he rolled to the playpen and picked up Desmond. "You're hungry, aren't you?"

He rolled to the kitchen and put Desmond in his highchair. There was spaghetti in the fridge, and he could open a can of green beans and heat them. Ed worked as quickly as his chair would allow, all the while talking to Desmond.

"I'll have this ready in a minute, son. Just hold on a little longer."

Desmond bit the cracker Ed had given him into small chunks and gurgled. He never took his gaze off his daddy, watching every move. When Ed lifted the pan of beans from the burner and poured them into a bowl, Desmond began patting his tray and smacking his lips.

"I'm coming," Ed said. He dished up a plate for Desmond and blew on it to cool it before preparing a plate for himself.

He sat and watched Desmond spoon the chopped bits of spaghetti into his mouth as rapidly as he could scoop it up.

Ed scowled. How much longer would there be food, and other bare necessities for his family, let alone money for a car?

There was only one thing he could do. The same old thoughts whirled through his mind. Kathy wouldn't approve, and deep down inside, he knew it wasn't a godly thing to do. He didn't understand how God could expect him to sit in this chair and not do anything to protect his family. Didn't Scripture say a man who didn't provide for his own family was worse than an infidel? Well, he was not an infidel, and he intended to do something just as soon as he figured out what that should be.

Ed waited for Desmond to finish his meal, and then he loaded the crotchety dishwasher and wheeled his son to the living room.

Ed picked up the yellow pages and thumbed to the auto ads. He jotted down names and addresses of small car dealerships. Then he thumbed over to the section headed "Auto Hand and Foot Controls." There were only four entries, and two had websites listed as well. He rebooted the computer and keyed in the first URL. He spent several minutes studying the options for hand controls.

Ed's heart began to race, and he had to wipe the perspiration from his hands. Transportation freedom was only a few hundred dollars away. Everything he needed was on that web page and the company who did the retrofitting was right here in Kansas City. They had lifts, chair tie downs, shoulder belts for wheelchairs, rotating seats, and even a special chair that could be rolled up to the dash and lowered to the appropriate height. There would be no need to move from a wheelchair to a car seat.

He could get everything he needed in one stop. Ed had to get the funds to do this. It was the only way he could keep his job. If things went well, he might even be able to take an evening job, too. There would be so many more opportunities when he had his own transportation.

He copied the phone number and made a call to one of the sales representatives. "I would like a general idea of what it would cost to retrofit a Ford van with hand controls."

The man asked several questions before he said, "I really need to have you come in and let us do an in-depth evaluation. I can give you a ballpark figure. Just don't hold me to it, if we have to make any special adjustments."

Ed assured the salesman he would understand if there were unforeseen considerations. He just wanted a general idea of how much money he had to have to even consider such a purchase.

As soon as Ed had that figure, he keyed in the URL for the casino. He had to get enough money to retrofit Kathy's van and buy her a smaller car. But Kathy must not know, at least not yet.

Over the next two weeks, Ed followed the same routine every evening. As soon as he got Desmond fed and settled to play, Ed went to his computer and set about trying to win enough money to reach his goal. He had several scary moments when he lost a large pot. He was always careful to keep enough to start again the next day. He had to win. Not winning was too horrible to contemplate.

Kathy looked more worn each evening. Neither of them mentioned what they hoped would be forthcoming at the end of the month. Ed was sure fear kept Kathy silent, and he certainly couldn't tell her what he planned until he had everything secure and in his hands. She would try to talk him out of his scheme, and he knew there was no other solution. He had to do this in order to feed his family. It wasn't like he was just doing it for fun. It was imperative that he get to work, and in order to do that he had to have a car. Owning a car required money, lots of it, and for the life of him, he could not see the "way of escape" the Scriptures talked about. So he really had no option other than to keep playing until he could pay for the alterations to Kathy's van.

He had no intention of losing Kathy and Desmond when he could do at least this much to keep things going.

Chapter 11

Ed dialed LaMont's phone number and waited while someone went to his room to get him. LaMont had opted to move to the dorm at the University of Missouri Kansas City campus, certain that environment would be more convenient than his former inner-city home.

"Yo, Bro," Lamont finally said. "What's happenin'?"

Ed jumped right in. "I need your help, LaMont. Can you come out here this weekend?"

There was a pause. "Maybe I could on Saturday afternoon. What's the deal?"

"Saturday afternoon won't work, LaMont. I need you to drive me to do some shopping, and we need the van. We'll have to take Kathy to work first."

"I don't know, man. What time does she have to be there?"

Ed ran his free hand over his head. "That's the problem. She has to report by eight, and we'll have Desmond. I thought you might come out on Friday and spend the night."

Ed braced himself for LaMont's groan.

"Man, your couch is way too short."

Ed actually laughed. He couldn't remember how long it had been since he'd done that. It felt good, and he planned to do it more often, starting right now. "You're right. There isn't a couch anywhere long enough for a soon-to-be pro-basketball player like you."

"What you talkin' 'bout, Bro? Nobody said I'm headed to the pros."

"It's just a matter of time," Ed said. "Before that happens, I still need your help, and just to sweeten things, I have a king-sized air mattress we can throw on the floor for you."

LaMont's hesitation made Ed's heart skip a beat. LaMont just had to do this. There was nobody else to whom Ed was willing to try to explain the situation.

Finally LaMont said, "If I come, you owe me majorly, man. I was goin' to ask Tamika Olivetti to the movies Friday night, and she is the dream girl of the century."

Ed laughed again, even though LaMont's tone made the situation seem like much more than a missed date with some good-looking gal. He sounded downright pitiful. "Maybe you owe me, little brother. I just saved you a good thirty bucks—and if your sappy whining means anything, I might have saved you thousands of dollars. Guys who sound like you wind up marrying gals like Tamika, and they can reduce you to paupers in a flash."

LaMont's voice sounded stern. "You can laugh, but I'm the one who'll be sleepin' on the floor while who knows who Tamika will be out with. All I can say is, this better be important."

Ed grew serious. "It is, LaMont. More important than you can possibly realize. I'll tell you about it Saturday—after Kathy goes to work, okay? All I want her to know is you're running me on some errands."

"Okay," LaMont agreed. "I can do that." His voice trailed off in a pensive sigh. "See ya' Friday night."

Ed chuckled again. "Thanks, LaMont. Just for the record, if you still want to ask Tamika out, I could leave the door unlocked and the bed ready. You could come in any time Friday night."

"Now you're talkin'. Thanks, Bro. I'll talk to you Saturday morning after I wake up."

Ed couldn't resist one last little jab. "Just remember, you could be stepping onto the path of a lifetime of financial commitment."

"Maybe," LaMont said. "For now, you remember, it's just a date. See ya' Saturday."

Ed hung up and sat contemplating their conversation. LaMont sounded really interested in this Tamika. It actually sounded like this was getting to be more than just dating. Ed wouldn't be so concerned if LaMont were older, but he was a mere freshman. He had four full years of college to go, and his scholarship didn't cover a wife.

Ed decided to let LaMont deal with his own problems. Ed had all he could handle right here at home for the moment.

Kathy drove as quickly as she could along Oak Street, and then north onto the Heart of America Bridge. She wanted at least a few minutes to talk with Ed before she had to report to her evening job. They needed to pray about their transportation problems. Kathy knew God held the answer, but she couldn't see any solution, and if Ed lost his job, they would be in such deep financial trouble she didn't know how they would recover.

There was always welfare, so they wouldn't starve. They also wouldn't be able to pay Ed's hospital bills, or even have anything beyond an existence. That made a bleak picture, but there were certainly even worse things than that if it went so far. She shook her head and chided herself. "Worry is a lack of faith. Get a grip, girl."

Kathy knew she needed to do exactly that, but she had no idea how. She drove through North Kansas City, and on up North Oak Trafficway to Vivian Road, where she turned right. After stopping to pick up Desmond, she drove to Antioch Road where she turned north. Now only a few blocks from their home in Meadowbrook, she began to pray in earnest.

God, you know our needs. You also know our limitations. I don't know what else to do. The hospital has been patient, and I know the physical therapists even worked for free, but everything Ed needed was so expensive. I don't mean to whine, but Lord, I'm tired. I'm really tired, and now this bus thing comes up. Show me what we need to do, and help me to be grateful for all the blessings we do have.

She continued her prayer all the way home. Unfortunately when she drove into the driveway, she still had no clue what more she or Ed could do to help themselves. She sat and dropped her head to the steering wheel as misery threatened to overwhelm her.

She didn't know how long she sat there before Desmond began to coo and call, "Mama, Mama, Mama."

Kathy sighed, lifted her head, and glanced in the rearview mirror at her son. He sat patting the restraining bar in front of him and continued to chant, "Mama, Mama, Mama."

Kathy smiled when Desmond saw her in the mirror and grinned broadly, then reached for her. "Okay, son. I'm coming to get you."

She grabbed her purse and went to release Desmond from his car seat. She glanced at her watch before she lifted him into her arms. In only a few minutes she would have to leave again, or she'd be late for her evening job. She grabbed the diaper bag and headed inside.

She pushed open the door and met Ed in the front hall.

He reached out to take Desmond. "I was coming to check on you. I was getting worried."

"I—" she paused, not wanting to admit to Ed how worried or tired she truly felt. She knew it was foolish for her to try to hide anything from Ed. He could tell her moods in an instant—at least he could if he paid attention. Sometimes he got so tied up in his own agenda that he missed a few things. If he really looked at her, he knew exactly how she felt without her saying a word. When they first got married, that made her feel transparent and vulnerable. As time passed, it made her feel very cherished and loved. Now, she was defensive and tried to hide her true feelings. It wasn't because she no longer wanted to share things with Ed. It was because she couldn't squelch her guilt for dumping even more problems in his lap.

Ed already felt guilty for "bringing all this load" on her, just as though he chose to have that mad man shoot him. Ed insisted he would never have been shot if he'd kept his mouth shut in the restaurant where they first encountered his shooter. Kathy had talked to Micah and Margaret, and all the guys who were with them. Ed hadn't said anything to warrant such a reaction. His paralysis and all the medical bills were not the result of Ed's actions. Instead they were because of a maniac committing a totally outlandish and illegal act of violence.

Kathy wished she could make Ed see he was not to blame. She also wished she could find some way to ease their financial problems. If it weren't for this transportation thing, they would have eventually dug out. Now, if Ed lost his job, she had no idea what they would do. She supposed they could file for bankruptcy. She was sure they would lose their home and the van as well. Then she would not even have a way to get to work. Regular bus service in the suburbs was sporadic at best, and the hours it ran didn't make allowances for stops at a babysitter's home.

Kathy sucked in a deep breath, and plunked Desmond into his daddy's lap. She saw the king-sized air mattress stretched across the living room floor. "What are you doing with that?"

Ed settled Desmond more securely on his lap. "I'm airing it up so you can put the bedding on it when you get home tonight. LaMont's spending the night, but he'll be here late. He has a date."

"Good for him," Kathy said, and then she dropped her coat and purse on a chair and headed to the kitchen.

"Get Desmond's coat off, then come on into the kitchen while I heat your dinner. We need to talk."

She pulled the large bowl of potato soup from the fridge and ladled some into bowls to place in the microwave. Before she made it back to the refrigerator, Ed wheeled Desmond to his high chair.

"What's up, Kathy?"

She grabbed the milk, and then moved to the cabinet to gather spoons and a box of crackers. "Ed, we need to pray about the bus service. Something has to happen to make them keep that van running."

She glanced at her husband, and it marveled her that he didn't look totally stressed over this mess. Usually things like this ate at him day and night, and he'd become angry and impatient. Tonight he looked almost peaceful. She didn't understand it. "So can we pray really hard right now?" she pushed.

Ed shrugged. "Sure, Kathy, we can pray. I just don't think we'll have to worry about it much longer. Things will get better soon."

Kathy sank onto a chair while the microwave did its job. "I certainly do hope so," she said, puzzled at where Ed's faith came from. Ed was a Christian, and she knew he believed in prayer. She was usually the one who did the encouraging. This was a new Ed, an Ed with more hope and faith. Maybe this long hard journey had been God's way of teaching them both to be less self-sufficient and more dependent on him. If so, it seemed to have worked on Ed, so now Kathy had to learn to "let go and let God." She wanted to do exactly that, but she wasn't sure how. Who was wise enough to decide the difference in doing your part and depending on God for the rest, or just saying "God take care of me," and not doing your part? How much was their responsibility and how much made it self-reliance? She certainly didn't know any more. If Ed's mood were any indication, maybe she could learn from him.

She reached out her hands, one to Ed, one to Desmond, and bowed her head. She listened intently as Ed prayed.

Father, we have a problem here, but you already know that. We've whined to you a lot over the past year. This time we're at a wall. Without a job I can't handle all these bills, and Kathy is already overworked, so we need an answer, and we need it quick, Lord. It's only another week before the bus service ends, and I can't afford to miss even one day of work, so we're depending on you to help us work this out.

By the time Ed finished the prayer, Kathy was calmer, but she still didn't see an answer to the problem. She guessed God just needed a little more time.

Chapter 12

Ed and LaMont drove Kathy to work the following morning, and then headed to Overland Park, a suburb on the southwest side of Kansas City, Kansas. Ed had called the shop again about having the van retrofitted with hand controls. He wanted to be certain it was possible before he bought a smaller car for Kathy.

The salesman at the shop greeted them and set to work interviewing Ed about his physical limitations. Then he went out to measure the van doors, head height. and door width. He returned to the showroom with a pad of copious notes and more calculations.

"We can work with your van with no problem." The man leaned forward and gave Ed's arm a pat. "You can even use your own wheelchair."

Ed glanced at the brochures with pictures of all the modifications needed. "How much will all this cost?"

The man named a figure that made Ed blink, but he had no choice. It just meant the car he hoped to buy Kathy would be a bit older and even smaller than he first planned.

"Can you have it all done by next Saturday?"

The man leaned back in his chair and blustered. "Well, I don't know. I'll have to special order the chair clampdowns, unless you want to move up to one of our motorized, adjustable chairs . . ."

"No," Ed said, intent on keeping the cost to a minimum.

"Then I can call in the order today. It'll take at least five days to get the lockdowns here, unless you want me to have them shipped overnight. Of course, that'll cost extra."

Ed did a quick calculation. If it took five days—even if Sunday counted as one of those—it would be Thursday before the clamps would arrive. "How long after everything is here would it take to install it all?"

"Depends on the work schedule," the man said. "Let me go see where we stand."

He left the room before LaMont said, "You're cuttin' it close, Bro. You better have that stuff overnighted, if you can."

Ed shook his head. "I need to save enough money to get Kathy a car." Even as he spoke it, he realized he would likely have to do as LaMont said. He couldn't afford to miss any work at all.

The salesman returned. "Looks like a bunch of people waited until the bus service is ending. We're booked solid from Wednesday on through the following week. If we could get the parts in here on Monday, we could finish you up by Tuesday evening."

Ed gritted his teeth, thought a moment, and then said, "Give me a total price for doing it that way."

The man grinned and moved to his calculator. After running the numbers twice, he gave Ed a final price.

Ed paused. He knew there was no other option, and unfortunately, the man sitting before him knew it, too. Finally he said, "Order the parts, and I'll have the van here early Monday morning."

"Excellent," the man said. "I'll order those right away, and all we need from you is prepayment of half the total cost. The other half will be due on Tuesday when we finish the job."

LaMont volunteered to call Hank, a college buddy, to come and drive them home, since they had decided to leave the van so it would be available as soon as the parts arrived. While they waited for Hank to arrive, Ed did some mental calculations about how much time they had before time to pick up Kathy.

Ed wrote the check while LaMont carried Desmond to Hank's well-used Chevrolet and buckled him into the car seat.

Ed wheeled to the Chevy and LaMont helped him in and stashed his wheelchair in the back. "Where to now, Bro?"

"Back up north," Ed said. "We need to hit the car dealerships along North Oak to see if we can find Kathy a little car."

LaMont drove onto the street, and then asked, "Who died and left you their fortune, man?"

"Nobody," Ed snapped. It wasn't any of LaMont's business where he got the money. He had it, and that was all that mattered. Besides, he couldn't explain in front of Hank.

LaMont glanced at his brother, but didn't ask any more. Ed was sorry he'd sounded so sharp, especially since LaMont had gone out of his way to help today. Still Ed didn't want to have to explain things. LaMont wouldn't understand. It was going to be hard enough to explain to Kathy, without anyone else asking a lot of questions.

Ed let a tiny grin escape. It might almost be worth explaining to LaMont to gain the practice for when he faced Kathy. She would be one tough audience, and he knew he would do well to be prepared or she'd shred him for breakfast.

Ed pulled his thoughts back to the task at hand. He had to decide how much money he had left to spend on Kathy's car. It wasn't near what he'd hoped he would have. He hadn't anticipated modifications to the van being so expensive, and he certainly hadn't anticipated overnight shipping charges.

What money he had left might buy a car, although it could end up being a junker. Kathy needed something reliable. She had to drive several miles every day, and he didn't want her sitting beside the road broken down all the time. In the first place, Kathy would be in danger; and in the second place, roadside repairs and tow services were expensive. He had to find something that would get Kathy where she needed to go safely.

They reached North Kansas City, and Hank headed up Burlington. He drove into the first dealership they came to, and Ed perused the lot. He saw very few used cars and all were large and fairly new. "I don't see anything here, LaMont. Let's go on up North Oak."

A salesman had started their way, but Ed waved him off and Hank drove on.

At the next dealership Ed spotted a tiny bright teal Contour. He wasn't that good at determining year models. He guessed it to be three to four years old. He pointed to it. "What do you think of that?"

LaMont shook his head. "Looks like a little blue roller skate. Even as tiny as Kathy is, I'm not sure she could fold up into that."

"Maybe," Ed said. "It would get great gas mileage, and I can't afford anything much bigger than that."

"What about an older used luxury car?" Hank asked. "They usually go sorta cheap."

"Yeah," Ed agreed, "but they guzzle gas like a hog slurpin' slop."

LaMont laughed and cuffed his brother's arm. "And just what would a city boy like you know about things like that?"

Ed shrugged. "I can read."

Desmond began to fuss, and Ed reached into the diaper bag for a teething ring. "We probably need to check his diaper before we go in," he said.

"I'll hand him to you," LaMont said. "He's your son."

Ed changed Desmond, and then LaMont wheeled them out of the car and down the long row of vehicles. When they reached the little teal Contour, Ed read the price on the window.

He stared at the sticker a long moment, reading features. It sounded like something that would work for Kathy. She would like the color, but it was too pricey. Ed knew he would be able to dicker and bargain and get the price down some. He hoped it would be enough.

A salesman approached, and Ed set his mind on how to get this car for a price he could afford.

The salesman greeted them. "She's a beauty, isn't she? We just got her in yesterday, and she won't be here long."

Ed knew the song and dance. He'd bought cars before. They discussed mileage, tire, and engine condition, and LaMont helped him in, and they took a test drive while Hank entertained Desmond at the dealership.

When they returned, Ed asked, "What's your absolute best price?"

The salesman sized him up, gave him a price somewhat lower than the sign on the window. It was still more than Ed could pay.

"No, man. I said your absolute best. I don't have a lot of time here."

The salesman paused, then said, "Let me go talk to the boss a minute."

Ed knew it was merely a delay tactic to allow him to drool over the car a bit longer. When the man did return, he said, "I'm sorry. That's the best we can do."

It pained Ed to let the car go. Despite all he'd done, he didn't have enough money, and there was absolutely no way he and Kathy could take on another payment, even if someone should be foolish enough to loan them money.

"I'm sorry I've wasted your time." he told the salesman. "I just can't go that much. Guess I'll have to look for a little less car."

The salesman nodded, and then asked, "Have you considered a Fiesta? We just took in a beauty about an hour ago, so we don't even have it cleaned up yet. If you're interested, I could take you to look at it."

"How old is it?"

The salesman perked up and started leading LaMont, Hank, and Ed to the garage as he spouted statistics.

When they reached the little car, Desmond began to bounce on Ed's legs and chatter, "Mine, mine, mine!" Ed laughed and held Desmond firm to keep him from toppling to the ground.

"The kid has good taste," the salesman said before he pulled the driver's door open for Ed to look inside.

The exterior was bright red and it had a soft dove gray interior. Although the vehicle was quite small, Ed was surprised at the leg room available in the front. He knew the back would be more limited. Fortunately, it would be several years before Desmond would need more than what was there.

"We took this in on a trade, and I can make you a real good deal," the salesman said. "The owner said he just put new tires on it last month and had a complete tune up at that time. She's in great shape. Why, there's not even any chips or scratches in the paint—and no salt damage, either. These folks just moved here from down south, so this car's never been through an icy winter."

Ed handed Desmond to LaMont and wheeled all around the little car. It was smaller than he would have liked, but the salesman was right. It seemed to be in perfect cosmetic condition. If it drove as well as it looked, Ed felt sure it would suffice for Kathy's needs.

"Do you want to take it out for a spin?" the salesman asked as he thrust the keys toward LaMont.

Less than an hour later Ed had written a check and arranged to pick up the car by mid-afternoon.

They went to have a quick sandwich and then returned to take ownership of the Fiesta. Hank drove Ed and Desmond to their house while LaMont drove the little red car. Before Hank left he agreed to return in a few hours to deliver LaMont back to the dorm, since LaMont would need to drive Ed to pick up Kathy at her job. Hank said he would also take Ed back to Overland Park on Tuesday evening to pick up the van.

After they got inside and had Desmond settled to play, LaMont looked at Ed and shook his head. "Man, you must be rollin' in dough. Now I know somebody died."

"Nope," Ed said. "Not yet, anyway." That would come after he tried to explain all this to Kathy.

Chapter 13

Kathy went to wash her hands, now that her shift had ended. She couldn't believe how tired she was. All she wanted to do was go home and go to bed. Unfortunately, once home, she would still need to get the family's clothes ready for tomorrow morning's church service.

She remembered the laundry was done, so she only needed to lay everything out for her two guys and herself. She sighed and dreamed of a day when they could afford the few extra dollars it would take to put new organizers in the closets so Ed could reach his own clothes. It seemed like such a small thing. It would be so liberating for Ed, and for Kathy as well. Kathy knew a couple of clothes rods and brackets wouldn't cost a huge amount, but the way their finances were, even a dollar or two would be missed. Clothes rods would have to wait.

She left the restroom and went to look for LaMont in their van. She reached the entry doors just as LaMont approached.

"Ready?" he asked, a broad grin on his face.

The grin seemed a bit exaggerated to Kathy. She chalked it up to LaMont's new status as a college freshman. Nobody else in the family had ever attended college, and LaMont's scholarship was a source of great joy for everyone.

Kathy nodded and asked, "Where are you parked? I didn't see the van."

LaMont took her arm and steered her across the lot. "We're not in the van. Come on, and I'll let Ed explain."

Kathy stopped. "Is something wrong with the van? Did you have a wreck?"

"No," LaMont said as he tugged her arm. "The van's fine and Ed will tell you about it. I'm not sure I could, even if I tried."

Kathy frowned and bit her lower lip. She allowed LaMont to help her into the back passenger side of the bright red Fiesta. "Ed, where's the van, and whose car is this?" She kissed Desmond's chubby hands. "Hi, baby."

Desmond smacked his lips and cooed, "Mama, Mama."

Kathy kissed him again, and said, "Well?"

Ed turned toward her. "The van is at a modification shop. I'm having it fitted with hand controls so I can drive myself to work, and this is going to be your car."

Kathy shook her head. "We can't afford all that, Ed. We can't even meet our bills now. They may even turn our power off any day. Have you lost your mind?"

Ed spoke over the seatback. "No, Kathy. I promise it will be okay. I have everything under control. Just relax and enjoy the ride home, and I'll explain everything when we get there."

"Yeah," LaMont pulled onto the street. "I'm driving you home, and a friend is meeting me there to take me back to the dorm. I have a date tonight."

Ed punched his brother on the arm. "You're movin' pretty fast there. That Tamika must be somethin'."

LaMont flashed his brother another broad grin. "She's a lady's lady, man. She makes me feel ten feet tall."

Ed laughed. "You are ten feet tall compared to all those other shrimps on the basketball court."

Kathy listened to the two men banter, aware it was a ploy to stop her questions until she and Ed were alone. They had an unspoken agreement never to fight in public, and apparently Ed expected a fight over the car.

Tears prickled Kathy's eyes, and she had to swallow twice to get the lump to go down in her throat. Ed had said he would be able to drive the van, and that would be wonderful. He deserved at least that much independence, and if he could drive himself, he would be able to get to work.

She glanced around the interior of the Fiesta. It was much smaller than the van. Even so, the three adults and the baby were not terribly cramped. Well, maybe LaMont was a bit scrunched, but he was tall. She leaned forward and studied the dashboard. It appeared to have all the basic amenities, and it didn't look too complicated. She was glad to see it had an automatic transmission. Ed had insisted she learn to drive a stick shift so she could handle any situation. On the hills of Kansas City she much preferred an automatic.

She ran her hand across the lush gray upholstery. It was a nice little car, and as cars went, she liked it well enough. But how could they possibly pay for it? She could not imagine how much the alterations to the van would cost, and this car seemed fairly new. Had Ed lost his mind?

LaMont parked the Fiesta in the driveway and went to get Ed's wheelchair from the trunk. Kathy unstrapped Desmond from his car seat and lifted him free. In moments they were inside and Kathy went to settle Desmond in the kitchen. He would be hungry soon.

She barely got Desmond into his highchair when she heard LaMont call out. "Here's my ride. See you guys later."

She heard the front door slam shut, and she waited for Ed to join her in the kitchen.

She offered a quick prayer asking God to help her understand and not to overreact. This boded to be a royal battle. She wanted to be reasonable and fair. She truly did not want to say or do hurtful things. She braced herself for the foray when she heard Ed's chair rolling toward her.

Kathy faced the door as he entered and waited for him to start first. Experience had taught her it often was not advantageous to attack before she knew all the facts.

Ed grinned like a naughty school boy, and that silly smile tugged at her heart. Still, she waited.

"I know you're worried about the money," Ed began. "That's the beauty of all this. Everything is already paid for—the van, the car, everything, so you don't need to worry about any of that."

Kathy stared at him a moment, trying to absorb what he said. It didn't make any sense at all. They didn't have that kind of money. Even before Ed was shot they couldn't have afforded all this.

She sank onto one of the battle-scarred oak barstools. "You're going to have to explain, 'cause I sure don't get it."

Ed paused just long enough to push her worry button again. "I've wanted to tell you, Kathy —well, I didn't think you would understand."

"Not understand what?" He should hurry and tell her, or her veins were going to burst from tension.

"I've been savin' money for several weeks, and I just yesterday got enough together to have the van worked on and to buy you that car." He rushed on while Kathy struggled with his words. "I know the car is smaller than you're used to. The beauty of that is it will use a lot less gas, and license tags and upkeep will be a fraction of what we pay for the van."

"That's all well and good, Ed," Kathy said, struggling to stay calm, "but where did you get any money to save? We've been struggling to row a sinking financial ship for months. There was no money to save. Where did you get it?"

Kathy barely kept the panic from her voice. She knew Ed had seen and heard many things in prison, and even in the neighborhoods there were people dealing drugs. Kathy didn't think she could stand it if she thought Ed was doing that. Deep inside she knew he wouldn't. Still, where could he have gotten all that money?

"Kathy, honey, I know this is going to sound bad to you. Just hear me out, okay?" He rolled his chair closer and took her hands. "You know how LaMont and I have played poker recently, and I told you how I used to play in prison?"

Kathy pulled her hands free. "You didn't win all that money from LaMont! He doesn't have that kind of money either!"

Ed captured her hands again, and squeezed gently. "Just listen, Kathy. No, LaMont doesn't have much money, but the casinos do."

"What casinos?" Kathy squeaked. "You haven't gone to any casinos."

"No, because I didn't have to. I won that money online." His eyes gleamed with excitement and his smile spread even wider before he pumped her hands up and down. "I beat the odds, Kathy. I beat them a lot of times. Everything I bought today is paid for."

Kathy jerked her hands free and jumped up from the old stool. "You *gambled* for that money?"

"Yes," Ed nodded, "and I won. Oh, I lost a few hands. I was real careful, Kathy. I never lost everything, and I won more than I lost. It has taken me weeks, but I got in the groove and I won!"

Kathy stood at the sink, staring out into the darkness. "You can't keep that money, Ed. It isn't right."

Ed smacked the table. "What are you talking about, woman? This is the answer to our prayers. How else am I going to get to work? And if I don't go to work, who's going to pay the rest of our bills. You sure can't take on a third job, and going on welfare won't help. We'd really be broke then."

Kathy turned and tears rimmed her eyes before she spoke. "I don't know how we'll cope, Ed, but this isn't right. God does not—and I emphasize *not*—reward sinful acts. God can and will provide what we need."

Ed's voice rose. "Who says anyone sinned? Show me in the Bible where it says not to gamble. In fact, the Israelites regularly cast lots. Wasn't that gambling?"

"No," Kathy almost shouted. "No, Ed, that didn't involve money changing hands, and Scripture says to do good to all men. Since when is taking someone else's money doing good?"

Ed didn't give an inch. "Oh, come on, Kathy. Those big casinos will never miss what little bit I won. They plan to lose some. It's part of the cost of their doing business."

"What about all the poor people who lost that money to them in the first place? Somewhere along the line someone suffers. I hear stories about people losing their businesses and their homes when they get caught up in gambling. What about those people, Ed?"

Ed's eyes grew dark. "That's not my fault. People who aren't careful and who don't know when to quit should know they're gonna lose."

Kathy sank onto one of the dinette chairs. "Ed, it's not right, and I think you know it. You need to return that money."

Ed rolled to sit in front of her and block her movement. "Maybe, maybe not, Kathy. You have to admit this win has helped solve at least one of our problems, and who should I give the money back to? The casinos? They'd just laugh at me, and it would mess up their bookkeeping with the gaming commission. They could be shut down for not paying out a patron's winnings."

Kathy ran her hands over her face. "Ed, it's still wrong. You know we're supposed to avoid even the appearance of evil. People who aren't Christians know all the sinful things that go along with gambling. The drinking, the sexy girls, all the stuff that undermines everything we believe in."

Ed frowned and shook his head. "I didn't drink, and the only sexy girl I've seen all this time is you." He grinned and winked at her. "I haven't left this house."

Kathy bit her lip and thought a moment.

Ed rushed on. "There's no way I can give the money back, Kathy. We need to just be thankful I won, and we could use the money the way I did. We can both get to work and have a way to earn enough to pay the rest of our bills."

Kathy drew in a deep breath. "I suppose so." She exhaled. "I still think God would have provided a better way. He promises we won't go without what we need. I still believe that. You used to believe it, too, Ed."

Ed stroked her hands. "I still do, Kathy. The book says a man who doesn't provide for his own is worse than an infidel. I'm providing the best way I know how."

"It's still wrong, Ed." Kathy searched her husband's eyes, and she saw them flicker. Was that guilt or was it anger? She wasn't sure, but she had to make him see.

"Ed, promise me you won't go online to the casinos again. God's promised he'll take care of us, and I know he will. Please, promise me."

Ed leaned back in his chair and sighed. "Okay. I won't go online to gamble any more."

Chapter 14

*W*hen Kathy wheeled Ed out to the red Fiesta the next morning, her emotions roller-coastered between pride and shame.

Nobody could deny the car was exactly what she needed, and she loved the color. It had pleased her when Ed told her the red would make her visible to other drivers, in spite of the car's diminutive size. She certainly didn't want to get run over, and the high gas mileage and low upkeep would be fantastic, just like Ed promised.

The problem lay in her unease over how to explain all this to their friends. She knew she wouldn't lie, even for Ed. Neither did she want to undermine him and the trust he'd managed to build with the church members since his conversion. He'd worked hard to win that trust, but it was fragile and could be destroyed very easily.

Kathy knew Ed's heart, and she knew he wanted to do what was right. Ed had learned his lesson about crime and sin, and he'd paid his debt to society. He'd also earned Micah's trust while he'd worked at the church. Before he was shot, Ed spent long hours cleaning and repairing the building, and he'd never taken anything that was not his, nor had he ever cheated on his time card.

Kathy also knew Ed would lay down his life for Micah, or Margaret, or for any of the other members for that matter. The church had always been there when the Johnsons needed them, and Ed and Kathy would never forget that.

Now, however, Kathy found herself needing to pull back and keep a secret from her brothers and sisters. It made her feel slimy and she didn't like it. No, she didn't like it one bit.

She went back into the house to carry Desmond to his car seat. She waited until she was buckled in and backing out the drive before she spoke.

"What are we going to tell Micah and Margaret?"

Ed glanced across at her. "We don't have to tell them anything."

Kathy stopped at the corner, looked, then pulled onto the main street. "Come on, Ed. You know they're going to ask where we got the car."

"So tell them we got it at the dealership on North Oak."

Kathy shot a scathing look at her husband. "You know they'll want to know where we got the money. They know how tight things have been since you got hurt. What am I supposed to say?"

Ed didn't answer for a long moment, and when he did, Kathy couldn't help the gasp that escaped her.

"I know you won't lie, so I guess you'll just have to tell them I won it."

"I can't tell them that. If anyone does, it will have to be you. I just can't do that to you."

Ed closed his eyes and leaned his head back on the headrest. "Okay. I'll tell them. I'll go forward and ask the congregation to forgive me and pray for us. Is that what you wanted to hear?"

"No," Kathy said, her hands white on the steering wheel. Then she added, "Yes. I guess that is what I want. I want us both to be right with God and with the church. I want to keep the respect we've worked so hard to build."

Ed's retort snapped against her. "We won't lose any respect, Kathy. Any man there will realize I did what I had to in order to protect you and Desmond and our home. They'll admire me for that."

Kathy shook her head. "You still don't get it, Ed. Your motive was good, but what you did was wrong. It won't do any good for you to ask for prayers from the congregation if you don't repent. You do remember what repentance is, don't you?"

"Yes, I remember. It's being sorry and changing your behavior, and I am sorry I got us in this mess. I've promised I won't gamble online anymore. What else do you want from me?"

Kathy glanced at Ed and saw the angry scowl, the knotted fists, and the rigid back. She reached up and wiped the single tear from the corner of her eye. "I want you to trust God to take care of us like he promised. I agree you need to do your part. Just remember it has to be without sinning. It won't do any good at all to make it through this life in comfort if we don't make it to heaven. I thought you knew that."

Ed smacked his hand on the dash. "I do know that, but I couldn't see anything in the Bible about gambling being wrong. I still don't, and I was trying to keep our heads above water."

Kathy turned off the freeway onto Highway 291. They were almost to the church and Ed still didn't understand. "You can't deprive other people and still please God. You have to keep yourself pure. Nobody is going to earn his way to heaven, and we can't prance in there with the filth of the world all over us, either."

She turned into the church parking lot and stopped at the handicapped entrance. Before she got out to retrieve Ed's chair from the trunk, he reached over and laid his hand over hers on the steering wheel.

"You're right, honey. I'll work on it, okay? I'll ask the church for forgiveness and we'll all pray, and I'll try hard to get it right from now on."

Kathy gazed into Ed's eyes and she could see he meant what he said. Her Ed was a good man at heart. He'd made a mistake, but he was sorry, and he was starting over. That's what God's grace was all about—allowing people to get up when they fell, and Ed wanted to get up.

"I'm glad," she said. "You know it's important."

"Yes, I know," he said.

He was true to his word. When the invitation song started, he wheeled himself to the front where Micah met him. Micah sat on a pew and they spoke to one another as the song ended.

Then Micah rose to make an announcement. "Brother Ed Johnson has come this morning confessing a lack of faith, and trying to handle all his family's problems without God's help. He admits that in that process he has been caught up in sin. He asks our forgiveness as well as God's, and he asks that we pray for him to be stronger in the days ahead."

Kathy fished in her purse for a tissue. Tears ran freely, and now her nose dripped as well. The tears were a combination of remorse over Ed's weakness, and a fierce pride in him for being enough of a man to do the right thing.

She knew how humbling it was for anyone to publicly admit wrong doing. For her Ed it was doubly hard. She knew she'd hit him with her strongest ammo when she'd talked to him about the respect they'd earned since they'd become Christians.

It hadn't been that many years ago that Ed, Kathy, and their families had been living in the ghetto, engrossed in much of the sin that abounded there. Only after Micah came to the prison and converted Ed and took him under his wing had Ed gained any sense of self-worth. That same transformation was true for Kathy and Ed's brother, LaMont, and his friends. Micah had given them the key to a better life, and up until now they'd used that key well.

Ed had fallen, but he was doing what it took to get back up and do what God expected. Kathy knew Ed would quit the gambling. They would cope somehow without it. God never failed in his promises.

Chapter 15

Before the service ended, Micah called the whole congregation to leave the pews, stand, and form a circle around the perimeter of the auditorium. Every member joined hands and they lifted their voices to sing "Love One Another" before one of the brothers lead a dismissal prayer.

Margaret had managed to stand on one side of Kathy, and Micah had Ed flanked on the other side. Margaret turned to the two and asked, "Can you come to lunch with us?"

Kathy glanced down at Ed, who nodded before someone came to clasp his hands and praise him for his courage and offer him encouragement to stay strong.

Kathy told Margaret. "We'd love to, but as you can see, it may be a while before we can get away." Kathy swept her arm to indicate the long assembly of people lined up to come and speak to Ed and to her to offer their love and spiritual support.

Margaret patted her on the arm. "Take your time. It will take me a bit to get things ready anyway, and this is important for you and Ed."

"Yes, it is," Kathy agreed. She turned to receive a hug from one of the widows of the congregation.

The little blue-haired lady hugged her fiercely and whispered, "It takes a big man to admit he's made a mistake. You hang onto him, Kathy. He's a keeper, and you help him keep right."

Kathy smiled through her tears. "I'm going to do my best."

By the time they climbed back into the Fiesta, Kathy was sure every member of the congregation had come to shake hands with Ed and to hug her. She'd never felt so loved in all her life.

She and Ed sat in silence most of the way to Micah and Margaret's home. Desmond, on the other hand, chattered all the way. "Quin-quin's house. Quin-quin's house." He couldn't say Quinthia, but he had part of it down pat, and he loved to play with the Forester's adopted daughter.

"I don't know if Quinthia will feel up to playing very much, so maybe we shouldn't stay too long," Kathy said when they pulled into the drive.

"Probably not," Ed agreed. "I think she gets tired really quick."

A lovely aroma of chicken and onions and celery baking together wafted through the room.

"Yum," Ed said. "Something smells really good."

Margaret had prepared baked chicken and dressing, green beans, a lovely German slaw, and hot rolls. Everything but the rolls was on the table by the time Ed and Kathy arrived.

"Desmond can go and find Quinthia in her room. The rolls are not quite done, and I still have to pour the tea," Margaret said.

"I'll help with that," Kathy offered.

Micah led Ed to the living room.

The women worked well together, and soon called the men and children to the table.

Micah waited until the children calmed, then prayed,

Father, we come at this time to praise you and to give thanks for all the many blessings you give us every day of our lives. We look at the world as a whole and we realize how very blessed we are. Even in our poorest moments we are rich, both in worldly goods and spiritual blessings. Thank you for that, and now especially thank you for our food we are about to enjoy. Thank you for the beautiful cook who feeds me too well, and thank you for our friends who are here to enjoy this meal with us. We offer this prayer through your Son, Jesus, whom we love and worship. Amen.

Kathy paused a moment and reflected on Micah's words. He was right. Even in their poorest moments they were richer than ninety percent of the world. What an awesome God they worshiped.

"May I serve you with the chicken and dressing?" Margaret asked. "I think it's too hot to pass around."

Kathy blinked back her musing. "Yes please. It looks really good."

As soon as everyone was served, Micah spoke. "I see you have a new car, Kathy. What happened to your van?"

Kathy paused and looked at Ed, expecting him to answer for her. He seemed inordinately busy with his chicken.

"It's in the shop," she said when Ed didn't look up. "Ed's having it retrofitted with hand controls so he'll be able to drive it."

Micah glanced at Ed, who had finally looked up. "Really? I thought cars had to be made that way at the factory. I didn't know they could retrofit them."

"Neither did I," Ed said, "until I got a brochure in the mail."

Margaret spoke, "That must be costly. Was the bus not working out?"

Ed shrugged. "It isn't costing as much as I thought, and the bus service ends the last week of this month. They're out of funds."

"I read that in the paper," Micah said. "I wondered how you were going to get to work. In fact, I'd already talked to Bruce about it, and we were trying to work up some sort of car pool. We almost had it together, too. I guess that won't be necessary now."

Kathy noticed the sick look on Ed's face when he heard Micah's words. When Ed had gone forward that morning, he obviously hadn't told Micah what his specific sin had been, and apparently Micah didn't think he needed to know, unless Ed chose to tell him. For Ed's sake, Kathy was glad he hadn't been required to list his sins, however, it might have been better if he had.

Micah went on. "We do have a discretionary fund that we might be able to use to help pay for some of those alterations. I don't know if it would be enough to cover it all, but we could help with some of it, I'm sure."

"No," Ed said, "we don't need any more help right now. The Fiesta and the work on the van are both paid for."

Kathy spooned a bite of dressing into Desmond's mouth, struggling to remain silent. It was up to Ed to deal with this, and she intended to let him.

"I see," Micah said, although he obviously didn't. "Then, I guess we need to be thankful for that, too."

Ed merely nodded and asked, "Could I have another roll, please? These are delicious."

Thus diverted, the conversation went on to other topics.

When the meal ended, and the dishes were done, Kathy said, "I think we should get home. Desmond and Quinthia both need naps."

"Yes," Margaret agreed. "Quinthia gets tired so easily. She does seem to be better, but the doctors are still concerned. Don't forget to keep her in your prayers."

"Always," Kathy agreed.

At home, Kathy put Desmond down before she returned to the living room where Ed sat waiting for her. She sat on the end of the old brown overstuffed chair and smiled. "I am so proud of you," she said.

Ed grinned and held out his hands. "I'm glad."

Kathy asked, "Did you hear Micah say the church was getting ready to help us? If you had just waited a little longer, God was working on the transportation problem for us."

Ed frowned. "Maybe so, but I hate taking charity like that."

Kathy drew back and studied him a moment. "Ed, it isn't charity in the way you're thinking of it. The word *charity* means love in the Bible. When Christians love one another, they help each other. We may receive that 'charity' or love this time. Next we could be the one giving the charity. When we love one another we can't allow ourselves to be too proud to give—or to receive. Sometimes it takes a greater love to let someone else give to us, whether it's money or time or service. Our pride is what keeps us from sharing that love in both directions."

Ed nodded. "Maybe you're right. All I know is, I want you to always be proud of me."

"I will be," Kathy promised. "You're a good man, Ed, and I'll always love you and be proud of you."

Ed squeezed her hands, and a light flickered in his eyes. "I think maybe we should take a little nap, too?"

"Now?" Kathy asked in surprise.

"Right now, my wife," he assured her.

Kathy gazed into the flame in his eyes and let it ignite one of her own. Her slow grin turned into a giggle before she rose, grabbed the handles of his wheelchair, and pushed toward their bedroom.

"I was wrong, Ed Johnson," she teased. "You're bad—really bad!"

Chapter 16

Things went well for several weeks. Ed got the van from the shop. He gathered Desmond and cautiously drove to a large parking lot on a Sunday afternoon. He practiced using the hand controls until he felt comfortable driving on the streets. It surprised him at how much the controls worked like operating a motorcycle. It was actually quite easy with only a little practice.

In no time he drove into the melee of downtown Kansas City with no problems beyond the normal frustrations of rush hour traffic in a large city.

Financially, things were extremely tight, but he and Kathy were able to manage. They never ate out, movies were a thing of the past, and even their everyday diet changed some. It was a bit of relief to realize they always managed to pay their bills. The one thing Kathy insisted they not cut back on was their weekly contribution to the church.

"God has given us everything we have, and we won't go without things we need, if we give like we are supposed to."

Ed knew Kathy believed what she said, but he could see the things they were doing without, too. Granted, they were not essential items, but they were living on a day-to-day basis. When he didn't respond to Kathy's statement, she continued.

"I know there are a lot of things we would like to have that we can't afford. We wouldn't be able to afford them even if we didn't give, and God certainly doesn't need our money. We give so the church can continue to teach other people, and to help others in need. Look around us. We have a house, clothes, and plenty of food. We both have jobs. Sure, it would be great if we could afford a few of the luxuries. Just remember God didn't promise we would have everything we want. Our wants would never end. He did promise we would have everything we need, and we do."

Ed couldn't argue with that. He couldn't think of a single thing they truly needed that they didn't have. Maybe Kathy was right. Maybe he just needed more faith. He knew they wouldn't always be in a financial hole. Some day they would have all his medical bills paid, and then things would be different.

In the meantime, Ed put out some feelers at work and at church, seeking an evening job for himself. He wanted Kathy to quit her second job and be the sitter for Desmond. She would be able to care for Desmond and catch up on her housework, too. She would be able to do things Ed wasn't able to, like the laundry in the basement, and picking up Desmond's toys, and the thousand other things she tried to do after working both jobs.

Ed had not said anything to Bruce, sure his boss would be offended if he knew Ed was looking for a second job. Bruce had gone out of his way to see Ed got the training he needed for his job, and he'd been more than fair with his pay scale. Ed's financial woes would certainly have been much more severe except for Bruce's intervention.

Although it should not have, it surprised Ed when Bruce stopped him one afternoon on his way out of the building.

"The grapevine tells me you're looking for another job. You're not getting ready to leave me, are you?"

Embarrassment engulfed Ed. He couldn't let Bruce think such a thing. He certainly couldn't do without his day job. "No way. This is the best job I've ever had, and I love it here. It's just that with all my medical bills, I need to work a few more hours."

"Good," Bruce said. "I was afraid I was about to lose one of my star employees."

"Not a chance," Ed said. "I would have come to you first, except you've already been so good to me, I didn't feel I could ask any more."

Bruce motioned Ed back into his office. He closed the door before he turned to Ed and asked, "How much more do you need, son?"

Ed hesitated a few moments. He didn't want Bruce's charity. Bruce waited, his gaze steady.

"My medical bills are way off the charts," Ed finally confided. "I need as much work as I can get."

Bruce motioned Ed to roll near his desk. "I was afraid of that. Has the insurance not kicked in?"

Ed shook his head. "Not near enough. I only had a minimal policy through the church. It was all I could afford. The deductible was huge, and it didn't cover any of my therapy. The doctors were very generous and wrote off quite a bit, but I still owe a huge bill."

Bruce sank into his leather office chair and steepled his fingers. "I know someone who might be interested in having you help him set up a program like ours. He's dealing with different products, and our software treatments will help his company get a competitive edge. It would be a temporary position. If I call him, would you be interested?"

"Absolutely. How long is temporary?" Ed knew the software inside out, due to Bruce's persistence. He could do this easily, and it would give him a little more time to hunt a long-term position.

"I'm not sure," Bruce said as he reached for the phone. "I'll call and ask."

When he finished his call, he said, "The assignment is for approximately four months. The pay will be what your salary averages per hour here, and if you want the job, you need to report to this address tomorrow evening at six o'clock."

Ed took the paper Bruce offered. He couldn't have asked for anything more perfect. The address was between the office and home. It wouldn't even cost him extra gas to get there.

"Thanks. Thanks a lot, Bruce."

Bruce rose and waved his hand in dismissal. "That's what a brother is for, Ed. When we love one another the way God wants, we do what we can. Sometimes it isn't much. At others, it is quite a lot. I hope this works out well for you and Kathy."

Ed gave Bruce's words some serious thought on the way home. It didn't take a genius to know the people in the church had helped him and Kathy in so many ways. He shuddered to think what would have happened if Micah had not loved him enough to come to the prison to teach him about God's love and salvation. What would have happened to LaMont and his friends if Ed and Micah had not gone to teach them, and then got them involved in the basketball league that won them all college scholarships? What would have happened to Quinthia's daddy if Micah and Margaret hadn't brought him to salvation in Christ before he died?

This love thing was still hard for Ed to understand. He knew he benefited, and he could see others did, too. What kept the love going? Didn't Christians ever get tired of loving other people? Hadn't Bruce done enough when he offered Ed a job, and not only that, but the avenue to learn how to do the job?

Apparently, Bruce didn't think so, for here Ed was on his way home to tell Kathy he had a new job.

"You what?" Kathy asked in surprise a short time later.

"I'm starting an evening job tomorrow," Ed said. "It's time I started carrying more of the load around here."

Kathy couldn't believe Ed had taken an extra job without talking to her first. "What about Desmond? We can't just dump him in the playpen and go off and leave him for the evening."

"Well, it won't be for long. I want you to quit your job as soon as you can."

Kathy turned and glared at him. "I can't do that. That won't get us ahead any at all. It just trades one income for another. We both need to keep working, so who do you have in mind for a sitter?"

Ed rolled his chair to pin Kathy against the wall, so she couldn't continue her task of pulling diapers and baby food from the diaper bag. "I know you want to help, and you can until you have time to give your boss some notice. After that I want you to be the one here with Desmond. You'll save us a lot by being able to do more here at home in the evenings. You can fix different meals instead of the quick stuff you have to use now, and you won't be so tired all the time. We'll only need a sitter for a couple of weeks at most. I'm going to make some calls this evening. I have a couple of leads."

"What kind of leads?" Kathy glanced at her watch, pushed past Ed's chair, and headed to the refrigerator to pull out the dinner she planned to warm for Ed and Desmond before she had to leave for her evening job. "We can't leave Desmond with just anybody. The papers are full of all sorts of horror stories about abusive babysitters."

"I know that. I'll be careful. You know as well as I do that we need me to do this. It's temporary—just a few months—but it can help us get back on our feet."

Kathy pushed the two plates she'd prepared the evening before into the microwave. "So who do you plan to call?"

Ed picked up the church directory from the kitchen counter near the wall phone. "Lacey for one. She'll know who in the congregation is looking for a job, and which teenagers have experience."

Kathy whirled. "I don't want some thirteen-year-old keeping Desmond every evening. He needs someone more responsible than that."

A frown covered Ed's face. "Not all teenagers are thirteen, and not all thirteen-year-olds are irresponsible."

"No," she had to agree. "I still want an adult. No teens, okay?" She searched Ed's face for some sign of agreement.

Finally, he sighed. "I'll try. That's the best I can say right now. Kathy, I can't let this job pass by. We have to get someone to keep Desmond, and they have to start tomorrow."

As soon as Kathy left, Ed went to the phone and dialed Lacey at home. He left Desmond in his highchair where his son sat gingerly picking up one green bean at a time and poking it into his mouth with studied precision.

"I'm sorry I couldn't call you at the office," he explained. "I didn't know I had this job until I started home this evening. The problem is, I have to find someone before tomorrow night, even if it is just for a few days. That would give me time to find someone for the long term."

Lacey's voice fairly bubbled. "Oh, Ed, what a wonderful problem to have. Now let me think."

Ed listened to the long silence before she said, "I can't think of anyone right now, Ed. All the teens are involved in some special projects right now." She paused, then went on. "Let me make an offer. If you don't find anyone else before tomorrow, call me at the office, and I'll come and keep him for you until you find someone. You did want someone at your house, didn't you?"

Ed hadn't given that question any thought until this very moment. "Well, that would be ideal. We wouldn't have to wake him to bring him home. I suppose if we had to take him somewhere else, we could."

"I thought it would be better, and too, I don't have any toys or anything to keep him entertained."

Just as Ed hung up, Desmond emptied his plate and squealed and banged his hands on the highchair tray.

Ed chuckled at Desmond's appetite when he wheeled around. "Okay, I'll get you more." He warmed another serving of the beans, along with a bit more of the chopped beef Desmond loved so well. Ed checked to be sure they weren't too warm, refilled Desmond's cup with milk, and then went back to the phone.

He flipped through the church directory to find Micah's number.

Micah sounded cheerful until his voice sobered when he told Ed, "I'm sorry, Ed. I wish I could help. I don't know anyone who would be willing to do it long term, and all the older teens we usually use are off in Mexico on a mission trip for two weeks."

Ed hung up and sat staring at his hands. He considered going through the newspaper ads, then tossed that idea. In the first place, he didn't have a paper. He'd have to go buy one somewhere. Even if he found someone willing to take Desmond on such short notice, it would be a stranger. He wasn't real comfortable with that, and he knew Kathy would throw a fit—well, not a fit. He'd never seen Kathy do that, but she wouldn't like it. He'd already heard her fears. He had to find someone.

It took some time before he realized he had absolutely no other resources to draw on, and he still had no solution to this problem. It took even longer for him to come to another conclusion. Kathy prayed all the time. Micah preached about prayer often, and Ed used to pray. That was before he strayed. He was ashamed now. How did you go back and face God after disappointing him like he had?

He clinched his fists and bellowed. "God where are you? Why don't you hear me? Am I such a slimeball you don't care anymore? I know I'm not much, but surely you still love Kathy and Desmond. What do you want from me?"

As soon as the words echoed away he slumped deeper into his chair. Sure, he'd repented and gone forward at church and asked the members to pray for him, but how could he face God and pray for himself? He was a spiritual nobody. God wouldn't care what happened to a weakling like him.

Intellectually Ed knew better, and he argued with himself.

You messed up, boy.

You repented.

You're still guilty.

You're forgiven.

You still did it.

God forgives and forgets.

I still remember.

You need him—especially now.

Ed swiped his hand across his face, and as frustrated and shameful as he was, he suddenly remembered a verse he'd heard. He couldn't remember where it was in the Bible, but he knew it came from Scripture.

"God's grace is sufficient . . . "

He couldn't remember the rest of the passage, but right here and right now, he knew this was all he needed to know. God would hear his prayers. Even after he'd made such a huge mistake, once he repented, God's grace would allow him to pray and be received.

Even with that knowledge, it was long after the kitchen was clean, and Desmond was in bed before Ed could bring himself to venture into a tentative prayer.

God, I need your help. I know I don't deserve it—he swallowed the lump in his throat—*but Kathy and Desmond do. I need this job, and you know we can't leave Desmond alone. We need a sitter. Please . . .*

His words trailed off into a whisper, and he dropped his head onto his arms which rested on the kitchen table. He'd done all he knew to do. Something or someone else would have to find the solution. He'd exhausted all his options.

Chapter 17

The morning didn't bring any miraculous answer to his feeble prayer. Kathy was ready to leave for work and Ed would soon follow, and they had no sitter, except for Lacey, who already had a fulltime job.

Ed handed Desmond to his mother. "Ask around at work. Maybe some of the people there will know someone."

"Okay," Kathy said, "and you can do the same." She started to the door.

Ed called after her. "I doubt that will do any good. My department is all guys."

Kathy turned around and flashed him an impish grin. "And none of them have kids who need sitters?"

Ed couldn't hide his surprise. "Well, I guess they do. I just thought since . . ."

Kathy laughed. She actually laughed out loud at him. "You just thought you were the only daddy in the world who helped with issues like this?"

"Well," Ed studied his feet. "I guess I didn't give it much thought one way or the other."

Kathy laughed again. "Oh, yes, you did. You feel sorry for yourself too often not to have given it any thought. I bet you'd be surprised at how many men there do make the sitting arrangements, or at least help with them. Just ask."

Ed groaned, then nodded. "Okay. I'll ask, but don't wager the farm on it."

The moment it left his mouth, he was sorry. Kathy's lower lip clamped between her teeth, and the worry flashing in her eyes told him much more than he wanted to know. "It was just an expression, Kathy, and you started it anyway. You said you'd bet there were involved guys in my office. Neither of us meant anything, okay?"

Kathy turned and opened the door. He heard the tremble in her voice. "Okay, but don't scare me like that again."

At the office, Ed did ask around. Unfortunately, none of the men knew a sitter who would be willing to work evenings. It did, however, surprise him to learn how many did, indeed, know the nuances of childcare. Kathy had been right. There were a lot more involved daddies than he had imagined.

By noon he had covered all the men in his department and even some others a couple of the guys suggested he ask. There didn't appear to be a babysitter anywhere willing to do evening sitting.

Ed reached for the phone and called Lacey. He hated to ask her to step in, but he had no choice. He had to start the job Bruce had arranged. He was sure he wouldn't be able to find anything else that would pay so well.

Lacey didn't hesitate even a moment. "Of course, I'll come, Ed, but I have another possibility, if you're interested."

Absolutely, he was interested. "Let's hear it."

Lacey's voice grew serious. "Well, did you meet my Aunt Zoe?"

Ed thought a moment. "The one who helped raise you, and the one Kathy has taken on as her personal project to try to convert?"

Lacey giggled. "Yep, that would be the one. Now bear in mind, I have not talked to her about this, yet. She told me earlier she would like to find, in her words, 'a little part-time job.' The only problem is, she's in a bridge club, she delivers meals on wheels, and she volunteers at the hospital. She can't fit a job into her daytime schedule, and she doesn't want to be out at night by herself."

Ed had hope there for a moment. Where was Lacey going with all this if Zoe didn't have time, or wouldn't be willing to drive at night. It wouldn't do Desmond any good.

Lacey continued. "I was just thinking. Aunt Zoe lives between you and me. If you or Kathy would be willing to take her home after you both got home, I could bring her to your house each evening. She wouldn't have to drive at all."

Ed gave it some thought. It would mean he or Kathy would be out later—or maybe not. They would have to transport Desmond if he went somewhere else, and it would be a lot more involved to take him than it would be to transport Zoe.

The idea grew on Ed. "Do you really think she'd be interested?"

"I'm almost positive she will be," Lacey said, "and I can assure you, she's great with kids." She giggled again. "After all, just look at how I turned out!"

Ed chose not to comment, although he agreed. Lacey was a very nice woman. "Do you have her number? I'd like to call her right away."

"Oh, you're at work. Why don't I call and talk to her about it, and if she's interested, I'll just bring her along tonight. Either way, she or I will cover this week for you. We won't leave you without a sitter for that precious baby."

Ed sank back in his chair and sighed his relief. "Thanks, Lacey. Kathy and I really appreciate it."

"No biggie," she said. "Now you get back to work and let me do the same."

"Yes, ma'am," he said and hung up. What a relief that was.

That evening, when Lacey dropped Zoe off, it was decided that Desmond would have the care he needed, and with both Kathy and Ed working two jobs, they just might be able to work their way out of this financial abyss.

Ed clung to that hope until the evening two weeks later when Kathy came home crying.

"Kathy, calm down and tell me what's wrong!" Ed demanded. He hadn't seen Kathy this upset since he's been shot, and he couldn't fathom what could cause this much distress now.

He glanced past her to the driveway, and her car seemed intact. It wasn't a car wreck.

"Did you lose your job?" He led her over to the old brown overstuffed chair and pulled her down to sit in it. He wanted to see her eyes.

"No," she sobbed. "It's nothing like that." She didn't say any more. She just sat and stared at her hands and sobbed.

"What, Kathy? What is it?"

She hiccoughed and then cried, "I went to see Dr. Hughes today."

Ed's imagination kicked into high gear. She'd said her eyes were bothering her. Was she going blind? He chided himself. Dr. Hughes was their family doctor. He would have sent Kathy to a specialist if something was wrong with her eyes. He'd heard her gagging in the bathroom a couple of days ago, and she'd been coughing some. When he thought about it, she'd only coughed that one Saturday when they'd pulled those dusty boxes down from the attic.

Fear gripped him in his chest. She had cancer. He could feel it in his gut.

"What, Kathy?" he demanded again.

She looked up, and tears splashed her hands. "I'm so sorry, Ed, but I'm . . ." She stopped, apparently unable to speak the horror she bore.

"Oh, Kathy." Ed leaned forward and pulled her into a hug. "It's okay, baby." But he knew it wasn't. God had dealt them another hit, and if Kathy should die, Ed didn't think he could stand it. It was one thing for Ed to have to deal with his handicap. It wasn't fair for Kathy to have to suffer, too. Anger boiled up, and he didn't have either the strength or desire to squelch it.

Kathy sobbed a few moments more, then leaned back and looked deep into Ed's eyes. "You're going to be a daddy again."

Ed blinked in stunned amazement. "I'm what?"

Kathy's tears continued to splash. "I'm pregnant again, Ed. We're going to have another baby."

Ed's anger vanished. "Yes!" he fairly shouted as he pumped one fist in the air. Almost immediately he sobered. "You're sure you don't have cancer, or some other horrible illness?"

She managed a weak smile. "Only pregnancy. I think that's more than enough! Oh, Ed, we can't afford another baby!"

Ed grinned. "Hey, baby, you're the one always tellin' me to trust in the Lord. We've made it this far, we'll make it from here."

Ed said the words, and he wanted Kathy to believe them. Deep inside he wasn't so sure. It seemed the harder they tried, the worse things got. When he took that evening job, he figured by the time it ended he and Kathy would almost have his hospital bills paid. He'd planned to find something for another six to eight months, and they would have been back on level ground.

Now, it would be much longer. Kathy's pregnancy with Desmond had not been all perfect, and Ed knew she wouldn't have the strength to carry this baby to term and keep her night job. Without that income, it would be over a year before they would see daylight again, and that didn't count the cost of her pregnancy. Thank God she had health insurance through her day job. At least their portion of the cost of the new baby would be minimized.

Kathy sobbed in his arms until it seemed there were no more tears left. He held her and stroked her, murmuring assurances. "Desmond will be the perfect age for a new brother or sister. He's gonna need someone to keep him from being a spoiled only child."

Kathy shook her head. "I wanted to wait until we had the hospital paid."

Ed noticed she never said, "Your bills." She had never blamed their financial problems on him, in spite of his name being the one that appeared on all those bills in the desk drawer. It shouldn't have ever been her responsibility to work all those extra hours in the first place.

"We'll manage, honey. Bruce told me today about another job that may open up when this one finishes. With your health insurance, there shouldn't be too much extra for us to cover."

Kathy began to cry in earnest again. "That's just it. My insurance has a pregnancy clause that requires the policy to be in effect for a full year. We're a month short. We have no pregnancy coverage."

Chapter 18

Ed had studied the problem for several days. This evening as he left his job to pick up Zoe and take her home, he again tried to determine some way to resolve all the money issues he and Kathy faced. There was no way that he could see. Absolutely none.

Ed's anger writhed and bubbled within him. He and Kathy tried so hard to get their finances under control and nothing they did seemed to make any difference at all. Where was God? Didn't he love them? What were they going to do now? Ed knew he'd made a mistake by gambling, but he'd repented. Things should have gotten better, not worse.

This should be a happy time. He and Kathy should be allowed to be joyful over this new baby. Instead, the news weighed so heavy Ed didn't think he could bear it much longer.

Kathy, on the other hand, had found the bright spot, once she got past her initial tears. "There is a clinic at Truman Medical Center that offers prenatal care on a sliding scale. I can go there, and I can keep working for most of my pregnancy. Neither job is all that hard. We'll be fine, honey. We just need to keep our heads down and keep working."

Ed loved Kathy even more for her outlook. He knew she was already tired. As the pregnancy wore on, she would be even more so. Kathy deserved some time off. He wanted to tell her to quit her job today, but that was impossible. There were way too many bills to indulge such thoughts.

He thought about going back to the computer. He'd won before. He knew he could do it again. He didn't need big pots. A lot of small wins worked just as well as one big haul. He could win; he'd already proved that.

It took longer than it should have. Eventually he shook his head and decided against gambling online. He'd promised Kathy he wouldn't do that, and how would she ever trust him again if he broke that promise? No, they would just have to keep on working. Somehow they would master this problem, but Ed knew it would take a very long time.

He parked the van in the drive behind Kathy's Fiesta and went to collect Zoe.

Kathy met him at the door. "I just got here. I'll take Zoe home, and I need to stop by the store for a few things. Desmond is already asleep."

Ed took a look at his wife and shook his head. "You're too tired. Give me a list, and I'll go."

"No," she insisted. "It will take you three times as long to get in and out of the van, and I know where everything is in the store. You'd spend an hour just finding everything."

She was right, but it galled Ed. He should be doing those things and letting her rest. Instead, he sat at home and she did all the errands, all the housework, and worked two jobs. What kind of man was he anyway?

"Fine," he ground out. "I'll make the lunches for tomorrow while you're gone."

"You can't. The fixings are what I need from the store. I forgot the lunch stuff Saturday."

Because you were so tired, he thought. But he knew voicing that would only make her more determined to prove him wrong. Instead, he found himself closing the door behind the two women as they left.

Kathy was thankful Lacey had suggested Zoe for the job. She was so gentle with Desmond, and yet she expected him to obey her. She was firm with the little boy, and yet she knew how to play and sing songs, and do lots of things to stimulate his learning.

"I'm so glad you're getting along so well with Desmond," Kathy said as she wheeled the little Fiesta toward Zoe's house.

Zoe clapped her hands in exuberance. "Now what is there not to like about that sweet baby?" she asked. "He is a delight."

Kathy laughed. "Ed and I think so, too, but he can be a little stubborn now and then."

Zoe chuckled before she replied. "Oh, yes, he can, but if it's channeled, that's a good trait."

Kathy cast her a doubtful glance. "I don't know so much about that."

"I do. Just take, for example, this evening. Desmond wanted to put a piece in that round ball of his with all the shapes cut out. He knew the star should fit, but he kept trying to put it in the other holes. Most kids his age would have given up after two or three tries. Kids his age usually have very short attention spans, you know, but not Desmond. He sat right there and kept trying until he got it to fit the right hole. That determination, or stubbornness, as you put it, led him to success."

"I see what you mean," Kathy said. "I think he must take after his dad in that respect. Ed never gives up, and since his accident, it is a good thing."

"It certainly is," Zoe agreed. "Lacey has told me how hard he worked to learn how to do the job Bruce offered him. His determination stood him well."

Kathy's smile spread. Her Ed was a special man, and she didn't need Zoe to remind her of his good qualities. She had to admit that it felt good for other people to be able to see his good qualities, too. She allowed herself a few moments of pride before she pulled her thoughts back to her goal for this trip.

She wanted to approach Zoe about reading Bible stories to Desmond before bedtime. Lacey had told Kathy that Zoe was a very good-hearted and moral woman, and Kathy had found that to be true. Lacey had also explained that Zoe firmly sidestepped any discussion Lacey tried to initiate about religion.

Lacey explained that Zoe was never rude or sharp, but she clearly was not interested in any extensive learning about God or his church.

Kathy wanted to try to stimulate some sort of interest, and she hoped and prayed Zoe might develop at least a little curiosity through Desmond's Bible story books.

She glanced over at the older woman whose eyes glittered with fun. "Zoe, I saw the story books by the rocker. Do you read to Desmond very much?"

"Yes," Zoe said, her smile wide. "He loves to be read to, especially when he's getting ready for bed. I just love reading to him then. He's so cuddly, and he is so cute when he points at the pictures and tries to name things."

A rush of pride filled Kathy's heart, and a touch of sadness swept over her. She wished she could be the one reading with Desmond every night. She only got to do that one or two evenings a week. She reminded herself she was thankful Zoe was able and willing to do it.

She glanced at Zoe again. "Have you read any from the Bible story books on the table by his bed?"

"No," Zoe said. "I haven't noticed those. All I saw were the books on the end table in the living room."

"Those are the ones he likes best during the day." Kathy glanced down at the speedometer and lifted her foot slightly. She certainly didn't need a speeding ticket. "I leave them out for him to play with and look at, since it wouldn't be a tragedy if they get torn or if he chews the corners. I keep the Bible story books up high and only let him see those when an adult can help him."

Zoe nodded. "I know what you mean. Babies don't intend to damage things, but they can be very destructive little dynamos if they're left to their own devices."

"Exactly," Kathy said. "I'd still like him to hear at least one Bible story every day. Will you mind terribly doing that for me?"

"Of course I'll do that, Kathy. As I said, I love reading to that little sweetheart. You said the books are by his bed?"

Kathy gave an inward sigh of relief. So far, so good. "Yes. There are several, and you can take your pick. Some have more pictures than others. For now, they may hold his attention longer, but you can use your own judgment."

Kathy parked in front of Zoe's house. "Thanks so much, Zoe, not only for agreeing to read the Bible stories, but for all you do. It means a lot to Ed and me to have someone we trust to keep Desmond."

Zoe had already lifted the door handle before she paused to pat Kathy's hand. "The pleasure is all mine, Kathy. I love having something to fill my evenings, and I already love your little boy more than you'll ever know. It's a good arrangement for all of us."

Kathy covered Zoe's hand with her own. "Yes, it is, isn't it?"

Zoe patted Kathy again, then slipped out. "See you tomorrow," she said before she closed the door.

Well, that certainly had been easy enough. Kathy realized just because Zoe agreed to read the Bible stories to Desmond did not necessarily mean Zoe would take any interest in them, but it was a start. If Zoe could just see some of the amazing things God had done, maybe she would be more open to exploring the Bible on an adult level.

Lacey and her friends had been praying hard for Zoe. Now that Kathy had grown to know Zoe, her prayers were more personal. You just couldn't love someone and not care about their soul. It hadn't taken long at all for Desmond to love Zoe, and Kathy would have loved Zoe for that alone. She had grown to love her for other things, too.

On that first night Zoe kept Desmond, as soon as he fell asleep, she must have gone through the house like a whirlwind. By the time Kathy got home, the kitchen was spotless, toys rested in the toy box, the bathroom sparkled, and the dryer sounded the end of the cycle for a load of towels and washcloths. Kathy had no doubt those would have been folded and put away if she'd arrived even a few minutes later.

Kathy tried to explain she didn't expect Zoe to do all that. The only thing she and Ed could afford to pay for was Desmond's care.

Zoe had brushed Kathy's words aside firmly. "I know what I agreed to work for, and there will be times when Desmond will take all my time—he sure can be active—but when he doesn't, I can do what I want to, can't I? I can read, or crochet, or watch TV?"

"Certainly," Kathy agreed. "That's what I had in mind in the first place."

Zoe lifted her hands to emphasize her point: "So, I can also decide to spiffy the place up, if I want to. Tonight, I wanted to."

Kathy laughed as she shook her head. "You shouldn't be working that hard."

"Nonsense," Zoe insisted. "I'm as sound as a horse, and I like doing housework. It's good exercise. Keeps the old heart pumping, and the limbs nimble."

Kathy had given up the argument, and Zoe had done as she pleased at least two nights a week, and some weeks even more. Zoe's help had been a real blessing, and it would be even more appreciated now that Kathy was pregnant.

She didn't want to admit it to Ed, but she grew wearier each day. She knew it was normal for pregnant women to crave sleep. It grew harder each day for her to concentrate on her job, especially right after lunch. Somehow she had to keep on keeping on. She had to. She couldn't let Ed down. "Help me, God," she prayed as she drove home from the grocery store.

Ed went to work each morning and Kathy didn't see him again until they both got home from their evening jobs. Kathy worried about her husband's stamina. He seemed to be handling things okay, but he was pushing himself way too hard so soon after he'd been released from therapy.

The doctors had said he was strong and healthy, except for his legs, and often enough Kathy had seen Ed do things that surprised her. In fact, she knew Ed's arms were probably stronger than most men's, because he used them to lift himself in and out of his chair, the shower, and his bed. Each move was probably equivalent to a pushup for normal men, and Ed must do over a dozen of those every day.

Kathy shook off her worry. She told herself worry wasn't a Christian thing to do, and she knew it. Worry was nothing more than greed and a lack of faith. She didn't doubt God could and would take care of them. She just wasn't sure he would do it in the way she wanted him to.

The whole thing was ridiculous. Either she believed God would take care of them, or she didn't. She had two jobs; Ed had two jobs; the bills were being paid, so she needed to lighten up.

One of the best ways she knew to do that was to plan a party. It would have to be small, and with her work schedule, and Ed's, she would have to find a time slot to fit it in. Not a problem. She could do something on a Sunday evening.

Kathy began to plan. She would ask Micah and Margaret, Lacey, and Zoe, and that new couple at church. What was their name? Lamcaster, Lambert, Lindstrom? That was it—Lindstrom. They had a little girl about Quinthia's age, and a boy about Desmond's age. That made how many? Eleven.

Eleven people sounded like a lot for their little house, but Kathy wanted all of those people to come, and she'd learned from some of the older women at church that it isn't how fancy you got. What did matter was how much you cared about people. She could show those folks a lot of care, even if her house was small.

She'd put the children at a card table, and somehow she would squeeze seven adults around her kitchen table, or maybe some could use TV trays in the living room.

That would work. She'd serve a veggie tray and finger foods, and everyone could find their own seating.

Perfect. Now all she had to do was plan a time. For that she needed to talk to Ed.

When she did speak to him in bed that night, it wasn't as simple as she'd expected.

"You don't need to be taking on any more work, Kathy. You're about to drop the way it is. It worries me to watch you dragging around here like you've shopped from here to California and back, and you're carrying all your bags by yourself."

Kathy rolled onto her back. "I am tired, Ed, but it won't take much energy to make a few sandwiches, open some chips, and slice some veggies. I can do it in the afternoon and still have time for a nap before we go back to evening worship services."

Ed snorted. "When have you ever taken a nap on a Sunday afternoon? You run to the store, you do laundry, you dust and mop. I could only wish you would take a nap."

Kathy rolled to face her husband. "That's just it, Ed. Now that Zoe is babysitting, she has taken over a lot of that stuff, and now that you have the van, I can send you to the store part of the time. I could probably take a nap. Even if I don't, I need this diversion. All work and no play wears Kathy down to a little nubbin." She patted Ed's face. "I need some fun, and truth be known, so do you."

Ed grabbed her hands and chuckled. "Maybe so, but are you talking now or later, woman?"

She giggled before she nuzzled close. "Both."

Chapter 19

It pleased Kathy that all her invited guests had accepted. She put Desmond down for his nap. Then she spent Sunday afternoon making ham and cheese sandwiches, peeling carrots, and slicing bell peppers, celery, and radishes for the veggie tray. Ed wheeled from the kitchen to the living room and back, asking for instructions on each trip.

"Can you manage the TV trays from the hall closet?" Kathy asked from the sink.

"I will, or die trying," Ed told her before he left the kitchen again.

"I don't want you to die," Kathy shot over her shoulder. "I don't even want you half dead, so if you need some help, call me."

"Yes, ma'am," Ed called back to her. She grinned for she knew he would do no such thing. She listened for the closet door's telltale squawk, then snickered when she heard Ed mutter about the mess of shoes on the floor.

He couldn't bend down far enough to reach them. Kathy knew he could reach the pair of extendable gripper tongs that hung on the inside of the door. They were just one of many pairs placed in strategic spots all over the house.

He could move the shoes himself, and she decided to let him. Still she listened to be sure he could handle the bulky trays.

It took longer than she'd hoped, before finally she heard the swish of Ed's chair rolling across the room, the solid thud of the trays landing on, she presumed, the sofa. A bit more muttering and she heard the clips snap into place on the legs for the first tray. Shortly, another and then another snapped.

It had taken a long time for Kathy to learn to let Ed work on his own, and certain things still came hard for her. She had to admit it was good for Ed to do as much as he could. It helped strengthen his muscles, not to mention how it eased some of her daily burden. Beyond that, it did wonders for Ed's sense of self-worth.

Kathy sent up a quick prayer.

Thank you, God, for being so good to us. Ed has learned to cope with his injury, and we're slowly pulling out of debt. I know Ed messed up, but he's doing good again. He's worried about the expenses for the baby, but I trust you to provide, and I'm even thankful this has happened. Desmond needs a brother or sister. Thank you, God, thank you.

She dropped the vegetables onto a glass tray, covered it with stretch wrap, and placed it in the refrigerator. Now what needed her attention? Table. She wanted to use that pretty flowered tablecloth Margaret gave her for her birthday, and she had yellow plates and cups and napkins she'd picked up at the paper-party store. She wished for cloth napkins and pretty china, but this would have to do. Besides, she reminded herself, it was the fellowship that mattered, not the trappings.

Ed wheeled into the kitchen. "TV trays all accounted for, and in place. What's next?"

"Chairs. I'll get the extra folding chairs from the garage."

"I'll help." Ed wheeled to the garage door. "Hand them in to me, and I'll set them up."

Kathy shook her head. "I don't want them in the kitchen. They need to go to the living room."

Ed sighed. "So, stack a couple here," he patted the arms of his chair, "and I'll wheel them in. You can bring the others."

"Got it," Kathy said. She did as he asked and then glanced around.

"What else, great chief," Ed teased.

Kathy brushed her hands down her pants, turned, and grinned. "Nap time. I'm done, you're done, and I am going to get a little rest before we go back to church this evening."

"Good," Ed said, his eyes serious. "I'll just read and listen for Desmond. If you hear him, don't get up. I'll take care of him."

"Thanks," Kathy agreed. "I am tired. I think a nap should fix me right up."

She slept until Ed shook her shoulder. "Hey, sleepy head, I hate to wake you, but it's time to get ready for church."

Kathy pulled herself from the haze of twilight sleep and murmured, "Is Desmond up? I didn't hear him."

Ed nodded. "He's been up over an hour. I have him all dressed. You have ten minutes before we leave."

Kathy enjoyed the evening service. Every now and then the song leaders were allowed a longer time for the song service, and they often taught the congregation new songs, along with singing the ones they already knew. Kathy and Ed both loved to sing, so those evenings were doubly enjoyable. This was one of those times, and it happened the Lindstroms sat beside them. They both had beautiful voices, and Kathy's heart swelled with joy as the whole congregation harmonized in a cappella praise.

Kathy knew the Scripture said to sing psalms, hymns, and spiritual songs, and to make melody in your heart. How could anyone not be joyful when they heard so many voices joined together to praise their heavenly Father?

They sang old favorites and, as expected, there was one new song. Kathy's eyes grew large and she nudged Ed and pointed to the attribution on the sheet of photocopied music each member had just been handed. Russell Lindstrom's name was listed as the composer.

Kathy turned and lifted one questioning eyebrow at the man beside her. He smiled, shrugged, and nodded.

Kathy had never known a song writer before, and when she read the words, tears sprang to her eyes. This man had put onto paper such powerful words about Jesus' life it took her breath away. Gratitude compelled her to offer another silent prayer of thanksgiving.

Thank you, Father, for giving us such a wonderful way to tell you how we love you, and to teach one another. And, thank you for giving men like Russell such special talent.

When the song leader led the first verse, a shiver ran up Kathy's back. This was what worship was all about: loving God, being thankful for his gifts, and telling him so. Kathy never tired of it, and this song was destined to be one of her favorites. The words spoke a moving message and the music was simple to learn and yet, beautiful.

In Kathy's opinion, there was absolutely nothing more beautiful than an a cappella song sung by a whole congregation, and Micah must have thought so, too, for when he stood to present his devotional for the evening, he talked about how moved he'd been when he first saw Russell's song. Micah proceeded to build a whole lesson on the theme of the song.

The service ended too quickly for Kathy, but there was still more joy ahead. She turned to the Lindstroms and asked, "Do you need directions to our house?"

Betsy Lindstrom patted Kathy's arm. "No, dear. I asked Lacey yesterday, and she drew me a very detailed map."

"Good," Ed said, before he reached for Desmond's diaper bag and set it on his lap. "Kathy is horrible at giving directions, and I'm not much better."

Russell Lindstrom chuckled. "It is good to meet a man who knows his limitations. A lot of people don't know either their capabilities or their limitations. Takes a wise man to manage either one."

"Thanks," Ed said. "I'll remember that. Now, if you'll excuse us, we'll go ahead and get ready for everyone."

Kathy slipped into the aisle. "Just take your time. It will take me a few minutes to get everything on the table. You'll want to meet some of the people here."

Russell and Betsy followed Ed and Kathy into the vestibule where they stopped. "See you in a few minutes."

Micah and Margaret, and Lacey and Zoe all knew the way, so Ed and Kathy rushed to the van, buckled Desmond in, and headed home.

"I'm glad you seem to have more energy tonight," Ed said.

"Yes," Kathy agreed. "The nap did me a lot of good, and having something besides work to look forward to helps, too."

Kathy watched Ed steer onto Antioch Road before he said, "I was afraid all the preparations would wear you down even more."

She gazed out the window a long moment before answering. Ed worried about her, and yet he was the one who sat in that wheelchair. He was the one who had to work so hard to do even the simplest things in life. If anyone should be worried about, it was Ed. Kathy had worked very hard to quit worrying about anyone or anything. She wasn't very good at it yet, but she intended to get better, and she wanted Ed to also.

"I'm not as weak as you seem to think, and besides, we can usually find the energy to do the things we really want to do. I want to have this party, and you, Ed Johnson, are going to quit worrying about me right this minute. You've already helped me get ready, and the ladies will help me clean up. I'm doing just fine."

Ed glanced over and winked at her, and her heart did that silly little skip-beat-skip thing it did every time he did that.

"You're doing more than fine, wife. You're doing stupendous." His grammar wasn't so great, but he knew how to make a woman happy.

They arrived home, and Kathy carried Desmond in while Ed followed with the diaper bag and their Bibles.

"I'll put things on the table," Kathy said. "You light the candles."

She giggled when Ed said, "Candles are for romance. How romantic can we be with a houseful of people?"

"Candles are for ambiance," she said. "Just light them, okay?"

Just as Ed blew out the match, the doorbell rang. He wheeled to answer it, leaving Kathy to finish her job.

Lacey and Zoe arrived first, and apparently had come together in Lacey's car. The Lindstroms came next. Russell carried the baby, and Betsy led their little girl inside. "Have a seat, everyone," Ed said. "Micah and Margaret should be along soon. Micah's usually the last one to leave the building."

"He has to speak to everyone," Kathy said when she stepped to the door to say hello.

In moments, Micah, Margaret, and Quinthia arrived. As soon as Ed had them settled, Kathy announced, "Everything is ready. We can eat as soon as we have our prayer."

She frowned slightly when Ed turned to Micah and asked him to offer thanks. Ed usually offered the prayer, but he'd been a bit lax the last few weeks. Kathy wondered if he felt uncomfortable praying since his gambling episode.

He shouldn't. He'd repented, and he'd asked forgiveness. God promised to forgive when approached by one of his children who was truly sorry for his sin. Ed should be able to go to God in prayer at any time.

Kathy chided herself. There was no reason for Ed to be the one to lead the prayer. Micah's prayers were effective. Still it made her wonder.

When Micah finished, Ed said, "Go help yourselves. Kathy has everything ready."

Kathy glanced over her shoulder as she led everyone into the kitchen. Ed had wheeled to the old boom box and put on a soft romantic CD.

After everyone had served himself and found a TV tray, Kathy couldn't wait to learn more about the Lindstroms. She plopped Desmond into the playpen and offered the highchair to the Lindstrom baby.

"What's his name?" Kathy asked.

Besty sliced a sandwich into thin ribbons and laid them on the tray. "His name is Jackie, and that's Carol." She pointed at her daughter and smiled.

Russell helped the little girl carry a plate and set it on the small table Kathy and Ed had prepared for the children.

By the time Kathy filled her plate and went to the living room everyone else was already seated and eating.

"I missed it," Kathy said to Betsy. "Did I hear you say you and Russell are opening a flower shop in Meadowbrook?"

Betsy laid her sandwich on her plate. "Yes, we are. It's sort of scary actually. We've never worked with flowers before."

Micah spoke up. "Really? I understood Russell to say you have a chain of donut shops in Springfield."

"We do," Russell said. We have businesses in other towns, too. We like to start a place from scratch, get it going, then find a good manager and move on to the next project. Betsy wanted to do a flower shop this time."

Kathy watched Margaret across the room when she smiled at Micah before she said, "How romantic. I remember when Micah and I went to buy our wedding flowers. It must be a lot of fun to help people with such joyous occasions."

"Yes," Betsy agreed. She grew sober. "Yes, it is great to help at times like that, and at the birth of new babies. I love to make corsages for the teen parties and anniversaries. Believe it or not, I even enjoy helping families when they're choosing funeral flowers."

Kathy frowned. "I'm not sure I could enjoy that. It's such a sad time for everyone."

"Yes," Betsy agreed. "That's why I like to help. It is a hard time and many of the stores try to take advantage of the 'guilt factor.' When death comes, it usually slips up on people, and at least some of the relatives wish they had, or had not, said certain things, and they tend to overbuy to compensate, especially if a clerk pushes them."

"How could anyone be that greedy?" Lacey asked indignantly.

"You'd be surprised how many are," Betsy said. "I like to get the family to talk about their loved ones and learn what's important to them. We've done some simple things and we've done some that would do the Queen of England proud. The ones I feel best about were the ones tailored to the person's life. We've done wreaths for a gardener that had lots of vegetables along with the flowers. We've done one with hammers, and pliers, and screwdrivers for a carpenter. Those are the ones that mean the most to the family, and not all florists take the time to help a grieving family make the most meaningful decisions. Most just want to get those hurt, emotional people out of their shops as quickly as possible."

Kathy spoke. "If you give all your customers that kind of personal attention, it won't take long for word to get around, and you'll have more business than you can handle."

"I certainly do hope so," Russell said. "Betsy's good with weddings, too. She's a stickler for giving the bride what she wants to make her personal dream come true, large or small. I've seen her do flowers for a wedding with eight bridesmaids and eight groomsmen for under fifty dollars, and it was gorgeous. Sparse but gorgeous."

"How in the world did you do that?" Zoe asked in obvious awe. "And why would you?"

Betsy chuckled. "I did it because that's all the bride could afford, and which florist do you think all those bridesmaids will use when they get married?"

"Smart woman," Ed said. "But that advertising must have cost you."

"Not really," Betsy said. "We just had to get a bit creative. Most people never think of gladioli for weddings, but it was summertime and the glads were huge and beautiful. We gave each girl one stem of a lavender gladiolus with a big bow and streamers to carry as an arm bouquet. We broke buds out of the tips to make boutonnieres for the men, and we used individual blooms from a couple of stalks to open and put back together in one big ruffled round bouquet for the bride. It was really pretty, within her budget, and the shop still made a small profit. It was a win/win situation for everyone."

Margaret nodded toward Kathy. "You two should get your creative heads together and talk. Kathy did some nice things for our reception, and she knew how to stretch our budget, too."

"I need that kind of creative input," Betsy said. "It isn't hard to sell the big weddings. Everyone wants the fairytale. Sometimes it is a challenge to make that happen for the young women with a limited budget."

"It sounds like fun," Kathy said.

"It is for me," Betsy agreed. She waved her hand at her husband, "But Russell can tell you it's a lot of hard work. Lifting buckets of flowers heavy with water, cleaning a cooler three or four times a week, making sure the delivery driver does his job on time without breaking any of the flowers—all of that keeps us hopping."

Margaret chuckled. "That must be what keeps you so thin, and I can't imagine working at a job I didn't like. You obviously are doing what you love. I can tell just by the way you talk."

Betsy ducked her head, embarrassment coloring her cheeks. She shot a glance at Russell. "You let me talk too much again."

"Not at all," Zoe said. "I for one find the whole thing fascinating."

"So do I," Kathy said. "I think I might enjoy that, if I just knew how to design."

Betsy's eyes lit up. "You can learn design, if you have any real interest."

"Oh, no, not really," Kathy said. "I already have two jobs, plus keeping the home fires burning. That's about all I can manage."

"Too bad," Russell said. "We're always looking for good help with some creative ability. That combination is hard to find."

Long after the evening ended, Kathy thought about what Russell and Betsy said. Working in a flower shop would be fun and rewarding. Unfortunately, she had all she could handle the way it was. Besides, she had no experience with flower design, and she couldn't imagine learning would be all that easy, in spite of what Betsy said.

No, it was better to stick with the jobs she had. She and Ed could not afford for her to give up a secure job to chase a new one that might not work out.

Maybe if they ever got Ed's hospital bills—and now hers—paid, then maybe she could venture out, but not now.

Ed sat at his desk the next day and muttered to himself, "It shouldn't be this way."

The sound of his own voice startled him, and he leaned back in his chair. Kathy shouldn't be stuck working evening after evening dishing up ice cream and making sandwiches. If she had to work, she should at least be able to do something she enjoyed.

He'd seen how her eyes sparkled when Betsy talked about the flower shop, and he knew Kathy would be good at designing, if she just had the chance to learn. He'd even talked to Kathy about it after everyone left. In spite of his best efforts, her practical arguments convinced him she needed to stay put at Frosty Freeze Ice Cream & Sandwich Shoppe.

Chapter 20

Ed felt a little better about it a few weeks later when Kathy came in one night and told him Lacey had asked Kathy to help plan a surprise anniversary party for Micah and Margaret.

Kathy moved around the kitchen preparing lunches for her and Ed for the next day. Her voice held an excited edge Ed hadn't heard in a long time.

"Betsy's going to help, too, and Lacey said we'll be working with fresh flowers. I imagine Betsy will do all that. Maybe I can watch and learn something."

"Sounds interesting," Ed said, although it really didn't. His only interest was seeing Kathy enjoying herself. Well, he did want Margaret and Micah to have a nice party. He didn't care who helped, as long as Kathy enjoyed herself.

Over the next couple of weeks, they both went to work and church with little diversion, except for the Sunday afternoon meetings which Lacey, Kathy, and Betsy held in secret.

One evening small baskets appeared in the garage, and when asked, Kathy explained. "I'm going to spray paint them blue, and we're going to put white daisies in them in something Betsy calls 'roundy moundy' arrangements. I don't know what that is, but guess I'll find out."

Ed lifted his eyebrows in resignation. "I suppose. When is this party going to be, anyway?"

"Not this coming Sunday, but the next. Lacey told Micah we've planned a potluck fellowship dinner that day. He has no clue we remember it's their anniversary."

Ed handed her the sandwich bags. "So what happens if he and Margaret opt out and decide to go to some fancy restaurant?"

"They won't," Kathy said with assurance. She took the mayonnaise and mustard back to the fridge. "Micah's the preacher, and he takes his job seriously. He'll be there whenever the church meets. If they do go out, it won't be for lunch that Sunday."

Ed knew Kathy was right. Micah was totally committed to the congregation, even when it meant making sacrifices with his own family plans. Micah was a good man, and Ed knew he would do well to try to copy some of that dedication. Ed had thought about that often in the past few weeks, and he intended to work on it harder every day.

On the Saturday prior to the party, Kathy gathered her blue baskets and headed to the church building. She left Desmond with Ed and went by the Hobby Lobby store to pick up some items Betsy needed.

Betsy was already at the building when Kathy arrived. "Good, you have everything. Come on downstairs and I'll show you what to do with it all."

Kathy watched as Betsy prepared the containers with floral foam and tape, then said, "Okay, I can do that."

"Good," Betsy said. "Once you get them all ready, dunk them in that five-gallon bucket. We want them really wet before we put the flowers in them. I'm going to help Lacey with tablecloths and runners until you get this stuff ready."

By the time Kathy finished with all sixteen tubs, Lacey and Betsy had finished their tasks. When the containers were soaked, Kathy placed them in the baskets she'd painted.

"Now for the flowers," Betsy said. "Watch me, Kathy, and you do exactly what I do."

"I don't know how to arrange flowers," Kathy said in a panic.

"I know that," Betsy said as she placed a designer's knife in Kathy's hand. "You can copy me. I don't have time to do all sixteen of these. You have to help."

Kathy took the knife, and shrugged. "Whatever you say. Just don't blame me if we have some really funny looking arrangements."

"I won't let you go too far astray," Betsy promised. "Here, Lacey. I have a knife for you, too."

"Oh, no," Lacey said. "I don't have a creative bone in my body. I'll go pick up the cake while you two do that."

Betsy eyed her a moment. "Oh, go on. We'll get this done in no time."

Kathy wasn't so sure, but it surprised her how easy it was to do what Betsy did, stem for stem.

"Not quite so short," Betsy said. "You want the flowers fairly deep in the foam so it can drink. Put that one right here, and it will be deep enough."

By her third arrangement, Kathy began to feel confident enough to work on her own.

"Go on, try it," Betsy urged. "We have plenty of flowers, and daisies are cheap. If you ruin a few, it's no biggie."

When she finished the arrangement, and it wasn't all lopsided or lumpy, Kathy couldn't wait to get home to tell Ed.

She still wasn't experienced enough to work in a shop. Still she was sure she could buy one of the inexpensive mixed bouquets in the grocery store and make a simple arrangement to take to someone in the hospital, or to a widow. It felt good to have learned a new skill, and she knew tomorrow Micah and Margaret would appreciate their efforts.

And they did.

The whole congregation stayed and the women brought platters of fried chicken, tubs of potato salad, cheesy casseroles, and homemade rolls. It was a feast beyond belief.

When everyone had finished, Russell rose. "May I have everyone's attention." He waited for the murmurs of conversation to end. "I'm fairly new here, but I've been asked to run this show, so here I am. Micah and Margaret, will you two come and join me over here?"

The two looked startled when they rose and came to stand next to Russell.

Russell looked at them, then turned to the congregation. "We're gathered here to wish Micah and Margaret a happy anniversary, and to be sure they have exactly that, we've put together a little gift for them."

Micah raised his hands and shook his head in protest. Before he could step back, Russell grabbed his arm. "Oh, yes, we do, and you have to accept it because we love you!"

Micah and Margaret looked at one another and then back at Russell. Neither offered to retreat again, as though in that one glance they'd reached a silent agreement.

Russell raised a light blue envelope into the air. "I've been told your wedding was blue." In an aside he said, "It's a woman thing." Then he continued. "You'll notice this envelope is blue, and when you open it, the paper inside is blue, but I think the words will put you in the pink, because this, my friends, is a gift certificate to the Basswood Bed and Breakfast for a mid-week retreat. Not only that, there's a certificate for free babysitting for Quinthia while you're gone."

"Speech," Ed called out.

Micah chuckled. "We didn't expect anyone to remember, and we certainly didn't expect a gift. I can assure you we will enjoy it."

Betsy moved to join them. "Enough! You've already preached one sermon. Now come and cut the cake."

Margaret helped serve, then came to sit with Ed and Kathy a moment. "Betsy says you helped make the flower arrangements, and I just wanted to say thank you. They're beautiful."

Kathy beamed. "They are, aren't they?" She glanced around, and in a somewhat surprised tone said, "I can't even tell which ones I did, and which are Betsy's."

Margaret agreed. "You have a natural talent, Kathy. You may just have to do something with that some day."

"Maybe now and then," Kathy said wistfully. "I'll never be able to work in a shop. I need to keep my 'for certain' job."

Kathy and Ed went back to work the next day and for the following weeks, until one fateful afternoon when Ed returned from lunch and rolled to his desk, ready to resume the afternoon's tasks.

A sticky note stuck to his computer screen caught his attention: *Call Kathy at this number. It's an emergency.*

Chapter 21

Ed's mind raced. The number was not familiar to him, and he wondered where Kathy could be and what would make her call him at work. She never called him here, because she didn't have time, and she knew if he was doing his job well, he didn't either. Something had to be seriously wrong.

He dialed the number. It surprised him when someone answered on the first ring.

"E-R . . . "

Confused, it took Ed a moment to realize he'd reached a hospital. His mouth went dry and his heart raced.

"Ugh, this is Ed Johnson, and someone left a message for me to call my wife at this number."

"Who is your wife, sir?"

Ed chided himself: *Get a grip, man.*

"Kathy Johnson. Is she there?"

"One moment, sir, and I'll check."

The woman put him on hold, and some syrupy music piped through the phone. Ed glanced at his watch: one-o-five. If he had to leave, he'd never get the afternoon's project done. He'd have to talk to Bruce and arrange for someone else to take over. Maybe it was just some minor thing with Desmond, a few stitches and he'd be okay. Ed could only hope. Even something that minor would require an insurance deductible to be paid. Ed ran his hand over his head. Were they never going to get control of their finances?

"Mr. Johnson, your wife is here," the woman said when she picked up the phone again, "but she can't talk at the moment. I'd be happy to have her call you a little later."

"That's fine," Ed said, "but what's going on, anyway? Which hospital is this? Is Desmond with her? Who's hurt?"

"This is Truman Medical Center. Just a moment, sir."

The woman took her time coming back. "Sir, your wife asked that I tell you she is the one being treated. She's being examined now, and will call you as soon as she can."

Ed didn't let her finish. "Is she okay?"

"I'm sorry, sir. I'm not allowed to tell you anything more over the phone."

"What department is she in?" he demanded. "I'm coming right over."

"You'll have to ask the receptionist when you get here, sir."

Ed reached for the mouse to shut off his computer. "I'm on my way."

As soon as he hung up and cleared his desktop, he went looking for his boss.

Bruce laid a hand on Ed's shoulder. "You do what you have to, Ed. We'll be fine here. Let me know how things turn out, and I'll be praying for both of you, and I'll call Micah for you."

"Thanks, Bruce," Ed said before he wheeled to the elevator.

Kathy was in the hospital. That meant she might lose the baby. It surprised Ed when a great sense of loss nearly overwhelmed him. He had to swallow a huge lump in his throat. He'd worried about how they would pay even just to get this baby here, let alone raise it. Now that they might lose this child, Ed realized how much he truly wanted this baby. Desmond needed a brother, or maybe a sister. Kathy wanted this baby, too. He'd seen the glow on her face after she'd recovered from telling him she was pregnant.

What happened? The question barely entered his mind before his face grew even grimmer, and he wanted to bellow his anger. Kathy had been working too hard, not getting enough rest, pushing herself—and he'd let her. What kind of man was it who didn't take care of his wife any better than that? The lowest of lowlifes.

He drove to the hospital as quickly as he could, all the while muttering at how long it took to get himself out of the van and rolled inside. Again, he was forced to accept that there was no way to hurry in a wheelchair.

Inside, he checked with the receptionist who sent him to the emergency room.

The nurse at the desk stopped him. "May I help you, sir?"

"I'm looking for Kathy Johnson. I'm her husband."

"Wait right here," the round woman said, as she rose. "I'll go see where she is."

Ed watched the woman waddle through the double doors. He waited as his patience wore thin. He wheeled back from the desk and over to where he faced those double doors. The minute he knew where to go, he would be ready. He wanted to be with Kathy. He needed to stay calm, and he wanted to keep Kathy that way. Yes. Calm was the ticket. Calm would make things better. Calm was their friend.

So why couldn't he quit fidgeting with the chair arms? At the rate he was going, the things would loosen and fall off any minute now. He had to get himself under control before he went in to see Kathy.

Deep breaths. That's it. Deep breaths.

The nurse pushed open the door and held it. "She's in the back, sir."

Ed pushed himself forward through the door and followed the maddeningly slow gait of the nurse to a cubicle to one side of the large emergency area.

Ed whisked the draperies open at one corner and moved inside. Kathy lay with her head turned away from him until he spoke.

"Kathy? Baby? I'm here, honey." Ed cringed at the sight of the IV and the monitors with all sorts of leads stemming from various locations on Kathy's body.

Kathy turned to look at him, tears glistening at the corners of her eyes. "I'm sorry, Ed. I'm so sorry. I didn't know what else to do."

Ed took her hands, again confused. What did she mean she didn't know what to do? Surely she hadn't—

"I had to come to the hospital," Kathy rushed on. "I know we can't afford it, but I didn't want to lose this baby, and when I started bleeding, I didn't know what else to do."

Ed let out a breath he hadn't realized he'd held. *Thank God, Kathy hadn't done anything to sabotage her pregnancy. Yes, thank God,* he thought again.

"It's okay, baby. We're going to be fine. I just want you and this baby taken care of. Are you okay?" he rushed to ask.

"I don't know," Kathy said. "I haven't lost the baby, yet, but I was cramping really bad, and I was bleeding. Dr. Hughes gave me some kind of medicine in the IV, and I'm getting sort of sleepy. They took a lot of blood, too. I don't know how long it will be before that comes back."

Ed was glad Kathy's own doctor was on call. Ed knew that if this hospital worked like most, the blood work could, and probably would take a long time. Fortunately, Dr. Hughes had a way of getting things done.

"You go ahead and go to sleep, honey. If they wanted you to sleep, that's what you need to do. I'll be right here."

Kathy gave him a wane smile, her eyelids already drooping. "What time is it?"

"Two-fifteen. Why?" Ed asked.

"Just don't forget to go get Desmond"—Kathy's eyes closed—"or call Lacey and ask her if she'll pick him up."

"She doesn't have a car seat," Ed said. "Where's your car?"

Kathy's words were barely discernable. "At work. Evelyn drove me here in her car."

"Go to sleep," Ed commanded. "I'll take care of it."

He sat at her side for quite some time and watched her sleep while rubber-soled shoes whisked to and fro just outside the draperies pulled around her bed.

In Kathy's cubicle it felt as though the whole world had stopped. The squeak of the rubber soles just on the other side of that thin piece of fabric reminded Ed that everything still progressed, oblivious to his and Kathy's personal crisis.

He held Kathy's hand and waited for Dr. Hughes to return. In the meantime he prayed. He wasn't sure God would hear his prayers, but he really didn't have anywhere else to turn. Even if God had given up on him, surely he would help Kathy. She hadn't done anything wrong.

At three o'clock he slipped his hand from Kathy's and wheeled to the lobby to find a phone and call Lacey. He'd just finished when Micah rushed through the entryway.

"Ed, who's hurt? Bruce couldn't tell me anything except that you were here."

Ed motioned Micah to a nearby waiting area, where Micah sat in order to be on eye level with Ed.

"It's Kathy," Ed said, struggling to speak around the lump that had risen in his throat again. "She may lose the baby."

Micah drew a deep breath and let it out slowly. "I'm sorry, Ed. That's a really tough one."

"Yeah," Ed agreed. "I didn't think it would be. I thought it would be a relief not to have to worry about paying for a new baby," he paused, "but it's not that way."

"No," Micah said. He leaned forward, elbows rested on his knees and hands clasped before him. "It's never easy to give up a part of us."

Ed shook his head and blinked down his emotion. "I need to get back in there. Dr. Hughes should be here soon."

Micah laid his hand on Ed's arm to stop him. "Let's say a quick prayer first."

Ed sank deeper into his chair, then nodded. He couldn't risk speaking right now for fear he'd crack.

Micah's voice was soft but firm.

Father, we're here today asking you to be with Kathy and her baby. You know what's best for all concerned, so we're asking you to do what Ed and Kathy need most. Give her doctors wisdom to use the skill you've given them and make her well . . .

Ed lost his concentration as Micah finished the prayer. He jolted upright when Micah said, "I'll be back this evening."

"Kathy would like that," Ed said, "and thanks, Micah."

By the time Ed returned to Kathy's cubicle, Dr. Hughes had returned with a colleague. "This is Dr. Fitzhugh. He's working with me for a few days."

Dr. Fitzhugh handed Kathy's doctor some forms. "Her blood work looks good so far."

Dr. Hughes glanced over at the monitor blinking and gurgling beside Kathy's bed. "The good news is the baby is still doing okay. We have a nice strong heartbeat so far, and you're not having any more contractions."

Kathy blinked and asked, "What do you mean, so far?"

The doctor shrugged. "Not all the tests are back, but everything we have looks normal. It looks like our biggest task is to keep everything the way it is."

Ed glanced at Kathy, then back to the doctor. "What do we need to do?"

Kathy's doctor flashed a big grin and spread his hands. "Nothing big. We just need to keep her off her feet for the next three months."

"Three months!" Kathy squeaked. "I can't spend the rest of my pregnancy in bed. I have two jobs to hold down."

Dr. Hughes shook his head and laid his hand on Kathy's shoulder. "Not if you want to keep this baby, Kathy. Your body is trying to reject it, and it will if we don't intervene."

Kathy looked at Dr. Fitzhugh, a silent plea in her gaze.

He shrugged. "I concur. You have to take it easy if you expect to carry your baby full term."

Ed gripped the arms of his chair in determination. "That's it, Kathy. I've wanted you to quit for a long time, and now you have to. We are not going to lose this baby."

"But how will we pay the bills?" Kathy wailed.

"I don't know," Ed said. "All I know is it won't be with your paychecks. As of this moment, you are a lady of leisure."

Kathy looked back at Dr. Hughes. "I can't stay in bed. I have a toddler at home, and Ed has to work."

Dr. Hughes didn't back down an inch. "I'm sorry, Kathy. If you want to keep this baby healthy, you must stay in bed. You'll have to find a sitter."

Ed's voice was firm, too. "You might as well give it up, Kathy. You are staying in bed until this baby comes."

It tore at his chest to see the tears flow down Kathy's cheeks, and he had no answer when she wailed again, "What are we going to do?"

Chapter 22

The first thing Ed did was call Micah. "They're keeping Kathy a day or two in the hospital. Before she is dismissed I have to find someone to stay with her during the day, and with her and Desmond in the evening while I'm working."

Micah's voice was full of concern. "Let me think about it a little. Right off the top of my head, I'd say Zoe might be willing to continue the evenings. Even if she agrees, that still leaves the daytime, but I'm sure something will come up."

Ed pinched the bridge of his nose. His head began to pound. "I sure do hope so. I don't see much help for this."

"We'll pray about it," Micah said. "We still have a couple of days. Actually, I'm sure Margaret and some of the other women at church would take turns staying until we can work on something more permanent."

That would give Ed a few more days to find a solution. Right now his brain seemed to have frozen. He could not think of one person who would be able to stay for three months, and even if they were willing, how would he pay them?

In the meantime, he went to work, visited with Kathy at the hospital on his lunch break, then picked up Zoe and Desmond and took them to his house before he went to his evening job.

That, too, presented a problem. The way things were, he could not get Zoe and Desmond settled and get back downtown without being half an hour late every evening.

Ed called his boss to explain about Kathy's near miscarriage and her projected long-term confinement. "I'm really sorry. Due to all this, I don't see any way I can get to the office on time as long as Kathy is confined to bed."

His boss listened patiently, offered his condolences, then said, "I'm sorry, Ed. You're a great asset to the team, but it wouldn't be fair to the rest of the men to delay them that half hour every night. As usual, we're on a deadline. I guess I'm going to have to find someone else, at least for this project. With the time crunch we're in I can't spare even a day or two to give you time to work out something else. If you still want to work after the baby comes, give me a call."

Well, that tore it. Everything Ed and Kathy had tried to accomplish was now flushed down the drain. Not only could they not pay the bills they had before, but now Kathy was piling up even more bills. Besides that, if she was having these kinds of problems now, no telling what else would pop up before the baby came. Ed replaced the receiver in its cradle and sat staring at his computer screen.

Now what?

To say Ed was surprised at Zoe's proposal as they drove home the following evening would have been a gross understatement.

"I've been thinking," Zoe said. "I was going to talk to Lacey about this, however I think what I have come up with today may be a better plan." Zoe's eyes sparkled as she clapped her hands together in excitement.

Ed couldn't imagine anything that would excite him right now, but he listened as Zoe continued.

"I've been wanting to have my kitchen updated for over a year, but I'm allergic to dust, and I'd start sneezing every time I even thought about all those saws buzzing and the hammers banging around."

Ed grinned. "Yeah. We guys sure can get a big mess going."

Zoe nodded vigorously. "Yes, you can. You know, I even went so far as to get estimates, pick the cabinet styles, and everything. Every time I thought I'd call and have them start, I'd think about how sick I would be while they worked."

Ed didn't see what Zoe was leading up to, but he nodded and listened politely as he drove up North Oak toward home.

"So, don't you see?" Zoe asked.

Ed gave her a deer-in-the-headlights look, and asked, "See what?"

"Well, I know you and Kathy might not like this idea, but it seems like the perfect solution to me."

Ed turned onto Vivion Road. "Solution to what?"

"Both our problems," Zoe said excitedly. "If I moved in with you and Kathy for those three months, I could put a twin bed in Desmond's room, and I'd be able to take care of Kathy and Desmond both. I wouldn't have to breathe all that dust and get sick. It just makes sense to use this win/win plan."

Ed glanced over at Zoe. He could not believe his ears. Zoe was actually suggesting she move in with him and Kathy. It would never work. He and Kathy couldn't begin to pay someone for twenty-four hour care, and he couldn't imagine anyone in her right mind even suggesting she share a room with a toddler.

He thought about it. Maybe they could put Zoe in the basement apartment. They still couldn't pay her.

He glanced at Zoe. "You're not serious, right? We can't afford that."

Zoe's face fell. "Oh, dear, I hadn't thought that far ahead. I know I move slow, and can't do as much as I used to, so I thought maybe the sitting might offset some of the expense." She paused only a second. "Still, I wouldn't expect you to keep me for free. I'd pay for my room and board, and your gas for taking me places. No, Ed, I'd expect to pay my own way."

Ed's mouth actually dropped open, and he had to consciously close it before he gathered his thoughts enough to speak. "You're suggesting you come and live with us, take care of Kathy and Desmond day and night, and pay us room and board? Are you crazy? You should be charging us."

Zoe glanced sharply at him, her brows raised in indignation. "Nonsense. I love Kathy and that baby. It will hardly be any work at all, and I'm the one who's being helped. I started to ask Lacey if I could stay with her, but she's still in that dinky studio apartment with barely room to turn around. That would never work."

Ed couldn't believe his ears. Zoe had actually convinced herself he and Kathy would be doing her a favor by letting her come and care for them for three months.

"Zoe, you know we need someone to help Kathy get through this pregnancy, and I can't think of anyone we'd rather have than you—"

"Good. That's settled, then. I'll have my bags packed tomorrow evening, and you can take my bed over tonight after you take me home. I've already moved it to the garage, and it's all ready to load." She flashed him a broad grin.

Ed scowled. "Letting you use the apartment in the basement would be a pleasure. You don't understand what I'm trying to say." Ed protested before he turned onto Antioch Road. "We can't afford to pay you for all that work. I wish we could, but I just plain don't have the money, and I have no way to get it."

"Pay me?" Zoe gasped. "What ever are you talking about? I absolutely refuse to move in rent free, and what little I'd earn for the little I do for your family wouldn't even begin to pay the rent on an apartment, let alone for groceries and transportation to who knows where all you'll take me. But I need to be in Desmond's room. I'm too old to run up and down your stairs all day long."

Ed shook his head. "Let me get this straight. If you move in, we won't have to pay you?"

Zoe glared straight ahead, her back rigid. "Certainly not. In fact, if you don't let me pay the difference in what I could earn and a reasonable rent, I won't come at all." She glanced over at Ed, her eyes flashing. "I didn't propose this arrangement just so I could sponge off you two."

"Whoa!" Ed said, struggling to smother a chuckle. "If anybody's being a sponge in this proposal, it's me and Kathy. You obviously don't know your own worth in the job market, but if you're serious, I agree this could help everyone involved. If we do this, nobody is going to pay anybody anything. Okay?"

Zoe studied him for several moments, and apparently decided he'd made his final offer. "Okay," she said. "We'll do it your way. Deal?"

"Deal!" Ed said, and one great weight lifted from his shoulders. It helped a lot, but there were still too many hurdles to jump for him to relax now.

Once he got Zoe moved in and settled, Ed began to seriously look for some sort of evening job. The newspaper didn't have many listings for part-time jobs, and the few offered were for manual labor. He wasn't too good to do that. He simply was not able from his wheelchair.

He called the state job service office, but they weren't much help, either.

"You might call some of the sheltered workshops in town. I can get you a list, if you're interested," the lady offered.

"No, thanks," Ed said. He'd contacted the workshops right after he'd been shot. They only offered day positions, and his job for Bruce paid better than anything they offered.

He called the financial office at the hospital where he'd been treated, as well as the one Kathy used, and explained his situation. Both case-workers were sympathetic and offered "easy payment plans." They didn't seem to understand—when the budget was already stretched to breaking, even an easy plan could be impossible.

Ed spent every odd moment trying to think of something he could do to help the situation. He told himself maybe there would be something in next week's paper.

He contemplated going back online to the casinos. He'd won before. Not just tiny pots, either. Hadn't he won enough to buy Kathy a car and to have the van retrofitted? He could do it again. He knew he could.

He chided himself for even thinking about it. He'd promised Kathy he wouldn't gamble online again. Yes, but neither of them had known Kathy was going to have to quit her jobs, and as a result Ed would lose his evening job. Still, he'd made a promise. He decided to wait to see if there might be an appropriate part time job listed in the paper.

There wasn't.

Time was running out. The mailman brought a new stack of bills every day.

He thought about the online casino again. It would be so easy to work the cards. No, he'd promised Kathy, and even if he decided it would be okay to break his promise under these special circumstances, Kathy would know. She was right there in the house, along with Zoe and Desmond, all the time. Even if Ed convinced himself it would be excusable to break his promise, it wouldn't be worth having Kathy go ballistic. She needed to stay calm and rest.

The other question he mulled was just how calm could she be worrying about the bills. He knew she wouldn't be able to just forget their money problems. She would fret and worry even more than he did.

One morning after again finding nothing listed in the newspaper, he went to the bedroom door. "I'm not coming home for supper tonight. I want to meet with some people about another job."

Kathy shifted on the bed and asked, "Do you have a lead?"

Ed didn't want to outright lie to her. He couldn't very well tell her his actual plan either. "I'm not sure, yet. I'm meeting with a group of people who may be able to help me. I may be late."

Kathy straightened her sheets. "I'll be here."

"Don't stay awake for me," Ed said.

Zoe carried Desmond to the kitchen. When she passed Ed, she said, "Don't you worry about a thing. We'll be fine. You just do what you have to."

"That's exactly what I intend to do," he said.

When he left work that evening, he headed for the Paseo Bridge, rather than the Heart of America Bridge he normally took. He turned east onto Highway 210, well on his way to the Ameristar Casino.

He'd promised Kathy he wouldn't gamble online; however, he hadn't promised he wouldn't go to the local casinos. He knew it was a fine line, and his conscience did sting, but he had to do something. He knew he could win at the tables. He had a real skill most people didn't have, and as he saw it, he didn't have a choice. He had to get some money somewhere.

He thought about how angry Kathy would be. He also considered how disappointed Micah would be if he learned Ed was gambling again. Micah had spent a lot of time teaching Ed what God's word meant for him.

Ed mulled that a moment before he pushed the guilty thoughts away. Didn't Scripture say something about a man who didn't provide for his own being worse than an infidel? He'd looked it up.

Ed decided he was choosing the lesser of two evils. He intended to provide for his family the only way he knew how.

There was no way he could have missed the turn off. A huge sign pointed the way, and even more signs directed traffic along the secondary road.

Large neon lights flashed at the entrances, and signs directed folks to various parking lots. Ed chose to go for the enclosed garage with handicapped parking.

He found a parking spot, lowered his ramp, and rolled out.

Although he'd seen casinos on TV and in the movies, he wanted to take his time and look around. He'd never been inside a casino before, and he needed to get his bearings.

The first thing that caught his attention was the extremely high ceiling that covered the whole complex of casino, restaurant, and small shops. The roof was painted pale blue with wisps of clouds here and there. It gave an amazing feeling of daytime outdoors. Unless a person looked at his watch, he'd never realize the sun had gone down.

Ed rolled down the center corridor which looked much like any mall courtyard. There were steakhouses, barbecue restaurants, even fast food places and an ice cream parlor. Right in the center of the corridor stood the entry to the gaming rooms.

Ed saw people lined up at the counter, and wondered if they were paying entry fees, or buying chips and tokens, or both. He decided to sit and observe a few minutes.

He then went to customer service. "This is my first time here. What do I have to do to get in?"

The hostess explained he needed a boarding pass and she took his information. "If you're playing poker, you can buy chips at the table," she told him as she handed him his pass. "Do you need someone to show you around?"

Ed considered that before deciding he'd prefer to explore on his own. "No, thanks." He rolled inside, deeper into the gaming room, and passed the slot machines, disdaining the foolishness of the people there. The slots required no skill or thought, save deciding how much money to toss away at a time, and a reasonably functioning arm to pull the lever.

Poker, on the other hand, allowed room for skill and intelligence. Sure, some of the game depended on luck, but as his uncle used to say, "Even a blind hog finds a few acorns."

It was knowing what to do with those "acorns" that made the difference in a winner and a loser. Ed knew how to leverage his luck with his skill and make money. He'd already proved that. Otherwise, he wouldn't even be here, he'd still be unable to drive, and he'd still be without the vehicle he needed.

He came here prepared to invest in his and Kathy's future and to make things better for his family, and he intended to do it now.

He came to the blackjack tables and stopped to observe a couple of hands. It intrigued him, but not like poker. After a few minutes he rolled on.

Ed wasn't sure how he would go about joining any of the card games, so he thought for tonight he would just watch.

The casino might not be too happy with him for not playing, but it was smart to make this a learning trip. Ed moved between the various tables, studying the protocol for each. He soon realized there were different versions of poker being played in various areas. Some of the versions he followed easily, others he had to observe longer to understand the differences in the rules.

Once he'd watched at several tables, he was fairly sure he'd seen all the variations. Obviously, he didn't know what they were called. He decided he needed to do a little more research. When he played online, he'd played Texas Hold'em, and that would probably be the game he would want to play here. He wanted to look over all the possibilities. He didn't intend to be like the average guy who just walked in and plunked his money down. He was going to play an intelligent game in an intelligent way. To do that, he needed to get back online and look up the rules for all the different games.

He decided to leave. On the way home he'd try to think of some way to keep his Internet research confidential. Kathy would never understand.

Chapter 23

*K*athy ran a pick through her hair and asked Zoe to bring her that pretty pink bed jacket the women from the ladies' Bible class brought her last week. Lacey had called and said she and Margaret were on their way over.

Zoe still hadn't offered the evening meal, and she seemed to be stalling for some reason. Kathy did wish she'd hurry.

When Zoe brought the jacket, Kathy asked, "Can we have sandwiches for supper, since it's getting so late? I'd like to be done before Lacey and Margaret get here so you can visit with them, too. I don't want them to rush off."

Zoe seemed to give it some thought before she said, "Lacey said she was coming by on her way somewhere, so I thought we'd just wait until they leave. I don't think we have enough bread to make sandwiches." She waved her hands in frustration. "Is that okay with you?"

Kathy supposed it would have to be okay since she couldn't get out of bed. Still, it disappointed her to learn Lacey and Margaret would be rushing off.

Zoe carried a couple of chairs in and set them on either side of the bed. "Thought they might want to rest after a long day," she offered before she rushed off to get another chair.

It seemed odd to Kathy that she would go to all that trouble if Lacey and Margaret were only staying a short time.

She didn't have the opportunity to give it much thought, because the doorbell rang just as she fastened the last button on the bed jacket. She picked up a mirror from the nightstand and smiled at her reflection. The top was feminine and pretty, and it fit perfectly. She knew a lot of care had gone into this selection, and she savored the feeling of being loved.

"Look at you," Margaret said when she entered the room, "all spiffy and pretty as a spring flower."

"You don't look bad yourself," Kathy replied after she'd taken in Margaret's light blue pantsuit. Then she noticed the basket Margaret carried.

Lacey followed close behind with another basket covered with a sunflowered napkin. Zoe followed Lacey carrying some TV trays.

"Now what are you three up to?" Kathy asked, suspicion mounting by the moment.

Zoe snapped one of the trays. "You can set your baskets on this." Zoe started out of the room.

Kathy caught her glance and frowned a question.

Zoe paused. "Well, you're stuck in here all alone, so we decided since you couldn't get out, we'd bring a picnic to you."

"Yes," Margaret said. "I brought fried chicken and potato salad."

"And," Lacey said, "I brought a green salad and cookies."

Zoe turned back to the door. "I have plates, napkins, and flatware, and iced tea. As soon as I get my tray of goodies we're ready to eat."

In an aside to Margaret, she said, "Ed said he and Desmond will eat in the kitchen, so we'll get them settled before we start. That way we can just chatter to our hearts' content."

Kathy scolded. "I thought you said Lacey and Margaret were on their way somewhere else."

Zoe clapped her hands and wiggled her eyebrows. "They are. They're going home from here. You don't expect them to spend the night, do you?"

Kathy wagged a finger. "You purposely deceived me. Shame on you."

"Oh, okay," Zoe said. "I didn't exactly lie, although I did sort of mislead you. I suppose it was wrong, but you pinned me down, and I didn't want to spoil the surprise. You know the old expression, 'Ask me no questions . . .'"

"And I'll tell you no lies," Kathy finished for her. "Okay, I forgive you."

Margaret set her basket on the TV tray and lifted the lid. The smell of fried chicken wafted through the room, and Kathy's tummy gurgled. She was hungry.

Lacey put her basket beside Margaret's. "I'll be right back. I just want to help Aunt Zoe get Ed and Desmond settled."

In only a few moments everything seemed to be under control and Ed rolled to the doorway, where he offered a prayer of thanks for the food.

Margaret filled a plate for Ed while Lacey fixed one for Desmond.

"I'm outta here," Ed said. "You ladies enjoy yourselves. Desmond and I are going to eat and then I'm going to work at my computer for most of the evening. Just make yourselves at home right here with Kathy."

"We intend to," Lacey said. "We have work to do, too."

"We do?" Kathy couldn't imagine what sort of work she could do from this bed.

Lacey slid onto the chair closest to Kathy. "We do. We need to make plans for the congregational homecoming to be held in just six short months, and we need your creative input."

Kathy grinned. "I'd love to help with that. I get so bored just lying here, and I can do all sorts of stuff for that."

Margaret handed Kathy a plate of food mounded high. "You most certainly can."

Kathy pushed the plate back toward her. "Not if I eat all that. I'd weigh so much I'd never be able to get out of bed. Put part of that back."

Margaret refused the plate. "But you're eating for two."

Kathy started laughing, then shook her head. "Margaret, you're showing your age. Doctors quit allowing that train of thought years ago. Now it's 'slim and trim' all the way." She extended the dish toward her friend again.

"Oh, all right. I want you to stay healthy so you can help with this project. We need you."

Ed wheeled himself to the kitchen. The sooner he and Desmond finished, the sooner he could get to his computer and do the research he wanted to complete before his next trip to the casino. He wanted to learn more about the protocol for playing poker in person as opposed to playing online.

Desmond was in no hurry at all, and Ed decided to clear his dirty dishes to the dishwasher while he waited. He knew to get online at a gambling site while Lacey and Margaret were in the house was risky. He decided he might learn more by doing a search on Google or Ask Jeeves. Surely some ambitious soul had written an article or two or had posted a website on how to play the various forms of poker.

Ed ran into several versions when he played in prison. There it seemed each person had one or two unique rules of their own. He wanted to be sure he knew how the casino played.

This was serious business for Ed. His and Kathy's future depended on the extent of his ability. He didn't worry much about his talent. He had a specially equipped van and Kathy had a car that proved he had a knack for the game. What he needed now was more knowledge and a little luck.

He decided Ask Jeeves might be most helpful, so he clicked on the URL, waited for the search engine to load, and then keyed in "poker rules." It surprised him to see how easy knowledge came to him when he got online.

More casino sites than he could count popped up, but there were a few that looked like they might have rules information. Soon he was deeply immersed in research. He found rules for Omaha Poker, Texas Hold'em, and others. He narrowed his search to Texas Hold'em. He knew that was the game used in the poker tournaments, so it made sense to expect the largest number of players at those tables. Everyone who played dreamed of being in the tournaments some day.

Ed knew he would never have enough money to enter a tournament even if he should want to, but he planned to get himself out of debt. Kathy and Desmond and this new baby deserved a better life than worrying from paycheck to paycheck. Ed didn't even want to be rich. He just wanted some breathing space.

He printed off a couple of pages of rules, then went back to Google and keyed in "casino protocol." He explored a few sites before he found a couple of articles that gave him the information he needed. He was ready. Tomorrow night he could start making his life, and Kathy's, a lot easier.

Chapter 24

*E*d waited until well into the day to say anything. He finally called Kathy. "I won't be home for supper again tonight, Honey. I need to check out another job. I want to stay and observe, so it may be really late."

"We'll miss you." Kathy's voice sounded so forlorn it tore at Ed's chest. It ate at him to see Kathy stuck in that bed day after day. He knew she had to be bored beyond belief. His Kathy was the bouncy, bubbly light of his life. Creativity gushed from her at every turn. Now all that had been shut down. Other than this small bone Lacey and Margaret had tossed her, all she had open to her was to read or watch TV.

Ed pounded the arm of his chair. Why had God let all these things happen to them? Micah said God was loving and took care of his people, so what happened here? Ed and Kathy had been faithful. Ed had even worked for the church as a custodian before he'd been shot. Kathy cooked meals for the sick, and taught one of the kids' classes. She'd organized fellowships and parties. Even now they seldom missed a service. That worried Ed, too. Kathy was supposed to stay in bed, but she insisted that if she could get up to go to the doctor's office for a checkup, she could get up to go to church for an hour.

Ed finally gave in, at least partially. "We'll go on Sunday morning and Wednesday night. That's it. I don't want you up twice in one day. You need to stay home on Sunday evening." Kathy hadn't liked it much, but she had eventually agreed.

He realized the worry wasn't good for her. Ed knew the bills bothered her every bit as much as they worried him. He thought about asking Zoe to hold the mail for him to go through first, but he and Kathy had always kept track of their finances together. If he suddenly took that away from her, he knew it would hurt her deeply. The last thing he wanted to do was wound Kathy any deeper than she already was.

He turned back to his computer. The sooner he finished his work here, the sooner he could head for the casino, and this time he was ready to play.

Ed rolled into the casino alert and eager to begin. He went to find a hostess. The article he'd read said he should tell the hostess what game he wanted to play, and as soon as a spot opened at the table she would seat him.

"I'd like to play three dollar Texas Hold'em," he told the pretty hostess.

"I'll check for a place," she said. "I'll need your initials so I can call you."

"E. J." Ed said. He watched her move between the tables. She had a bristly sort of class, as though the day-to-day work here had scuffed all her smooth edges. She looked hardened, with her smile fixed on with Super Glue. She would still be smiling even if the casino slid off into the river and sank.

Ed looked away. He didn't want to think about things like that. He wanted to concentrate on game strategy and winning. He had to win, and he couldn't allow anything, even sympathy, to distract him.

Yeah, he admitted to himself. He felt sorry for that woman. She probably had a family at home who depended on her wages to make ends meet. Couldn't she find a job that didn't eat away at the soul?

He was doing it again. He couldn't think about it. He had to concentrate, and besides, who was he to judge when he was here, too. But he didn't intend to make a career here. He just wanted to make enough to pay his bills, and then he was out of here for good.

He glanced around, then decided to buy himself a soft drink.

"Can I put a little kicker in it?" the waitress asked.

"No, thanks," Ed said. He didn't drink, and even if he did, tonight would not be the night. He needed a clear mind.

The waitress brought his cola, and he watched the crowd. The slot machines sat to his right and he watched as a group of people fed the gluttonous machines. Two white-haired ladies sat side by side, playing the nickel slots. Ed grinned when he realized they fed their machines at a slower pace than the younger patrons around them.

One lady methodically counted out a dollar's worth of nickels and laid them in front of her before she picked up each one and dropped it into the slot. It looked to Ed as though it took every ounce of strength she could muster to pull the handle after each deposit.

Time and again the woman leaned forward and squinted at the spinning wheels, leaned back, glanced at the lady next to her, shrugged, then reached for another nickel.

What a waste, Ed thought, except those ladies probably knew they wouldn't win. They were looking for companionship, and if it meant coming to the casino and sitting by someone with like needs, so be it.

Ed thought it was a shame they didn't find that companionship in church; then he almost laughed out loud. How consistent was that thought with what he was doing here? He didn't want to think about that, either. This was not a pleasure trip for him. He had work to do.

He sought the hostess again, and when he caught her attention, she motioned for him to follow her.

She led him to a table at the far side of the room and pulled a chair back so Ed could roll close. The men at the table nodded and introduced themselves.

"Hanes," the man to Ed's left said. He was short and heavy, and he guarded a smoldering cigar with his right hand. The others continued around the table.

"Franks." He wore a cowboy shirt and bolo tie.

"Gordon." This man dressed sharp, and his eyes were piercing. Ed decided he would probably be a player to be reckoned with.

As soon as introductions were completed, Ed purchased a hundred dollar's worth of chips. It pleased him to see his stack matched or outranked the other player's stakes. He should be able to hold his own without having to buy more chips, at least for a beginning.

Ed watched closely as the small and big blinds were posted. Ed received an ace and a king of hearts, and he decided to raise the bet. The flop turned up a jack, another ace, and a king. He raised again.

Franks and Hanes folded, and Gordon raised.

The dealer showed a six of hearts at the turn.

Gordon hesitated only a second before he raised. Ed read the hesitation as a sign of indecision. He called and raised again.

The river was a king. Ed had a full house. He'd won.

For these small stakes, it didn't amount to a lot of money. What mattered was he'd proved he could do this and win. As soon as he had a little more money, he could move up to the higher staked games.

Smug self-satisfaction engulfed him. He was still the man! He decided the next thing he needed to do was check out the other casinos in town. He wanted to know whether or not there were better games with better odds elsewhere.

Over the next few weeks Ed had to come up with various excuses to give Kathy to explain all the time he spent at the casinos. He also needed to explain the erratic income from his winnings. Some evenings he won quite a lot. Others, he lost or barely broke even.

Ed didn't want to totally lie to Kathy, yet he couldn't tell her the truth, either. It took some hard thinking, but he finally settled on telling her he had a job and was paid commission rather than a set salary. It wasn't really a lie. Ed considered his trips to the casino a job. He didn't go there for pleasure, although he did enjoy the rush of winning. That elation was heady stuff, but the reason Ed went in the first place was to win enough money to get back his and Kathy's normal lives. The glow from winning was just an added bonus.

Things went well for a few weeks. Ed expected to lose now and then, and he did. To his delight, mostly he won. His winnings began to accumulate, and he thought he soon would be able to pay his hospital bills and then he could start tackling Kathy's.

The problem was, the baby was due in two more weeks. Ed needed to have this project completed by then. He wanted to be with Kathy when they brought their new child home.

They still didn't know whether they were having a boy or girl, because Kathy insisted they couldn't afford an extra discretionary sonogram. Ed had to agree with her, and it irked him. It didn't matter to him which they had. Either way it would be wonderful, as long as it was healthy. He could wait to see which they had. What irked him was that he couldn't pay for the extra test, even if he had needed to know.

A man should be able to pay for the things his family needed, and have a few extra dollars here and there. Ed grimaced and vowed, *We will have. It won't be this way much longer.*

Chapter 25

$\mathcal{K}$athy didn't understand it. Ed came home late each night, and he told her he'd been working, but she never saw a paycheck. Every now and then Ed told her he'd been paid some sort of commission, and he made small deposits in their checking account. The ones Kathy saw reflected on the bank statement she held in her hands wouldn't even cover the expense of driving to a job. Why would Ed spend so much time for no more benefit than this? It didn't make sense.

When Kathy asked him about it that evening, he explained. "Kathy, learning a job takes time. You don't make much at first, but eventually it gets better. I'll start making more soon."

Kathy listened, and what he said made an odd sort of sense. She still didn't understand what Ed was trying to sell. When she asked again, he paused long enough to make her even more curious.

"It's sort of an investment program" he said. "It's complicated to explain, and I'm too tired to try," he told her.

Kathy knew Ed had to be exhausted, so she quit asking and let him get ready for bed. That was the least she could do, since she couldn't contribute anything else to benefit their financial status.

The next morning Margaret called. "Hey, girl, I just wanted to tell you our good news!"

Kathy smiled at Margaret's cheerful voice. "So spill it," she said.

"Quinthia's in remission. Thanks to the new doctor, they're hopeful it'll be long-term this time. Her blood counts are looking good."

"That's wonderful," Kathy squealed. "Thank God for that new doctor, but are they sure?"

"No," Margaret said. "There's no way they can be, but they are optimistic."

Joy rushed over Kathy. Quinthia was such a darling little girl, and she was so young. She deserved this reprieve from sickness and possible death. Margaret and Micah deserved this good news, too. They should be allowed to see Quinthia grow up healthy and happy.

"I'm so glad for you," Kathy said. "I needed some good news."

Margaret's voice grew concerned. "How are you doing, Kathy?"

The question came at a time when Kathy's spirits sat at the bottom of the well. "I'm fine physically," she said, "but I'm sort of down this morning."

"Anything in particular bothering you?" Margaret asked.

Kathy pleated the edge of the sheet. "Not really. It's just a combination of stuff. Money's tight, as usual, and Ed's gone all the time, and I'm stuck in this bed. Zoe's having to work herself down to a frazzle looking after Desmond and me, too. I'm even having to face the possibility of not having Dr. Hughes deliver the baby. Apparently he's retiring and selling his practice to Dr. Fitzhugh. If I don't deliver right on time, Dr. Hughes won't be there." She sighed. "I'm just in a whiney mood."

Margaret moaned. "Oh, Kathy, I'm sorry, but look at it from the perspective of Dr. Fitzhugh's being younger and probably a lot more knowledgeable of newer techniques. That could be a good thing, especially since you're having problems."

"I know," Kathy said, "and I know it's silly to fret and whine. Every once in a while I seem to need my pity party."

Margaret replied, "Well, you have a right to whine a bit, but not for long. Things will be better after the baby comes and you get back on your feet. One reason I called was because I thought you might be feeling a little housebound."

"That barely touches the hem of the garment," Kathy groused. "What I wouldn't give for a good old coffee klatch, or a party, or something."

"What a great idea," Margaret said. "Are you up to a come-and-go baby shower?"

"What?" Kathy exclaimed. "Here? Are you serious?"

"I certainly am," Margaret assured her. "Lacey and I can set up cake and punch in your kitchen, Zoe can help you with the gifts, and you can see and talk to everyone as long as you please, right from your bed."

Tears gathered in the corners of Kathy's eyes, and she swiped at them with her thumb. "You'd do that for me?"

"Of course we would, silly. You'd do the same for anyone else, and we'll do almost anything as an excuse for a party!"

Kathy thought a moment, then protested: "But I don't know whether we need boy things or girl things."

Margaret laughed. "No, but you do know you need company right now, and you're going to need diapers, and formula, and baby food, and lotions, and ointments, and vitamins, and tons of other stuff. If we provide those things, you'll be all set if you have another boy; and if you have a girl, it's a given none of the little old ladies will be able to resist bringing you frilly dresses and pajamas, even if they have already given you a gift."

"I'm speechless," Kathy said. "The people at church have been so good to me and to Ed—"

"So say yes," Margaret interrupted. "I thought Saturday afternoon would be good, if that would work for you."

"Have you talked to Zoe?" Kathy asked.

"Yes. She says she's ready to get you smiling again."

Kathy couldn't suppress a laugh before she said, "In that case, I guess it's Saturday afternoon. I'm certainly not going anywhere."

When Ed heard about the shower, he told Kathy, "I'll make myself scarce while you party." The last thing he wanted was to be stuck in his small house with a bunch of chattering women. Besides, while he had a legitimate reason to be out of the house for an extended time, he could go back to the casino.

He had a sizeable stake now. If he found the right game, and played his cards right, it might be his last trip to the boats. If he could maximize what he already had, he could quit gambling.

Losing was not an option. He had to win.

On Saturday morning, Ed decided to leave early. Margaret and Lacey were due at nine-thirty to decorate and do whatever women did to get ready for a gig like this.

Kathy had no problem with his leaving, but she did wonder where he would be for all that time.

"I might go find LaMont," he told Kathy, purposely leaving his answer vague. He hadn't said he would find LaMont. He merely said he might. He might not, though. In fact, he wouldn't be able to if he were to accomplish what he intended in the time he allowed himself.

Ed went to the kitchen to make sure Zoe had everything she needed.

"Yes, we're all set," Zoe said. "You just go enjoy yourself. You deserve a break, too."

Ed blinked and caught himself just short of saying, "Maybe, but I'm going to work."

Thank goodness he hadn't made that slip. He would never have been able to explain just what work he intended to do on a Saturday.

He rolled to the van, locked his chair down, headed down Chouteau Trafficway, and took Highway 210 to the Ameristar, where he wheeled into the parking lot. He took a deep breath, checked his wallet to be sure of the exact amount he had, then headed inside. This was it. This was the day he planned to earn his and Kathy's freedom.

He went straight to the poker room and bought five hundred dollars worth of chips. He gave the hostess his initials and told her he wanted to be seated at a twenty-to-forty-dollar Texas Hold'em table. While he waited, he mentally figured how much more he needed to win. With the table's limited wagers it might take him quite a while, if there were several players. His watch was broken, and he knew none of the casinos had clocks displayed. He would just have to estimate his time. He didn't want to get home too late.

Soon the hostess called his initials, and he moved as quickly as he could to follow her to the designated table. As usual, she pulled the empty chair away to allow him to roll closer.

He set out his chips and took a deep breath before he schooled his entire body to subjection. This was no time for him to betray himself to the other players with some nervous "tell."

Good players studied their opponents for subtle tells, and when they discovered them, they used them like weapons.

Knowing what a tell looked like, and when they were fake to throw an opposing player off track was one of the talents cherished by good players, and coveted by the poor ones. Ed prided himself in being able to read most players accurately. It was one of the things that made him such a successful player.

The dealer lost no time parceling out the first hand, and Ed was on his way. He cast all his concentration into the game, and he won the first round. That surprised him a little, since he hadn't had time to study the other players.

The win had been dumb luck. The next would require more work on his part. When his turn came, he placed his bet and studied the players as they placed theirs.

There were six other people at the table, and by the end of the third hand, Ed had won almost a hundred dollars. He knew the lady on his left rubbed her nose when in doubt, the lady next to her rubbed her right index finger on the edge of the table when she held good cards, and the man next to her sucked in his right cheek ever so slightly while he planned strategy, which meant he had a mediocre hand.

The next man leaned back in his chair before betting the maximum. He wanted the others to think he was undecided, but his eyes were clear, and he never blinked. He knew what he was about.

That left the two little old ladies on the end. Ed almost felt sorry for them. It was obvious to anyone who wanted to look that they came to be around other people, and they didn't care if they won or lost, as long as they had a good time along the way. They both smiled broadly and snickered at good hands and frowned and looked worried at poor ones they chose to fold.

It bothered Ed to take their money so easily, but they didn't seem to mind. Besides, if it did matter to them, they should either learn to play better or go to the slots and stay off the tables.

He soon realized he should have saved his thoughts, for in a few short hands, those two expressive little old ladies held the majority of the chips on the table.

Ed knew their tells, but he'd been dealt lousy cards, and somehow he'd misread the women. Those two little old ladies were far from innocent novices. They were playing out deceptive signals and cashing in.

Ed refused to allow any outward sign of emotion, but on the inside he seethed. Those two had scammed the whole table with their little skit. He was on to them now. At his next turn he watched closely, then he announced, "Raise."

He had a nine and an eight of hearts. The flop turned up a queen of hearts, a two of diamonds, and a ten of hearts. All he needed on the river was a jack of hearts. He knew chasing a straight of any kind didn't make good gambling sense, but he was only one card away from a straight flush. Those women were crazy, and their luck couldn't hold. All the other players folded, so it was between Ed and the two blue-hairs. Let the little old ladies beat his hand if they could.

The one closest to him folded, just as he expected, but the other one frowned, looked at her hand again and said, "Raise."

She pushed in a wager that lacked only twenty dollars taking all Ed's chips.

He didn't hesitate. She was bluffing. She had to be, and Ed needed that pot. He pushed his chips out on the table. "All in."

The river was the jack of hearts Ed needed for his straight flush, and it took all his strength to keep from gloating. The old lady couldn't beat that.

But she did!

Her original cards were a king and an ace of hearts. With the flop she held the king, queen, ten, and an ace, and the river had given her the jack for a royal flush.

She took the pot, including the remainder of Ed's entire stake!

He excused himself from the table, more than a little shaken. He'd been stupid and let a couple of old women break his concentration. He'd lost sight of good judgment. As a result, he'd lost a good portion of what he'd worked so hard to gain. He told himself everyone lost now and then. It wasn't in the cards to win every hand. He knew that, and he just had to pick himself out of the dirt and get back into another game.

He rolled to the teller's cage and gave the hostess his pass and asked for another five hundred dollars in chips.

"I'm sorry, sir. There's a five hundred dollar limit per two-hour session in Missouri."

"I know," Ed said. "My watch is broken, and I can't find a clock. How much time before I can buy in again?"

The hostess checked her computer screen. "Looks like an hour and twenty minutes, sir."

Ed drew back in shock. It had only taken forty minutes for him to lose five hundred dollars. He needed to get back into a game before another hour and twenty minutes. He wanted to get this job done, and the sooner the better.

He rolled around the perimeter of the casino. He knew it would do no good to try to cajole the hostess into selling him chips any sooner than she'd designated.

The gaming commission was very strict about the laws. They had personnel and cameras in every casino in the state. It could cost the casino its license if it were caught allowing a patron to exceed the five hundred dollar loss limit per two-hour session.

Ed's mind whirled. He had to win his losses back, plus make a good-sized profit by the time Kathy's party ended. Sure he'd left home early, but he didn't have any time to waste.

The Ameristar wasn't the only casino in town. He'd drive to Harrah's. They were only four or five miles down the highway, and he'd be able to get back into a game as soon as he got there.

Unfortunately, when he arrived, the hostess told him they did not offer poker. They did have poker machines, and they had a blackjack table, as well as baccarat.

Ed didn't feel comfortable with his knowledge of baccarat, and although he had averaged well with the online poker machines, he felt he might be able to bolster his purse quicker at the blackjack table.

"I'll take five hundred dollars worth," he told the teller before he went to scout out a table. He wanted to watch a game before he actually played. Ed had played blackjack before, but it was somewhat different here. Even so, he was sure he could handle it.

The first thing he noticed was the smoke that clouded over the table. He would have to remember to hit the shower as soon as he got home, or Kathy would jump on him like a duck on a June bug. He studied the game and noticed the players did not verbalize their bets. Instead they used hand motions, and the entire game was played in silence. After watching a few hands he was ready to play.

He rolled to a table with an empty seat and placed his chips, careful not to put them inside the betting area.

The dealer dealt him two cards, both face up, then went around the table giving each player his hand. Ed held a ten and a two. The dealer's showing card was a seven, and he chose to stand.

At his turn, Ed motioned for a hit. The dealer sent him an eight, for a total of twenty. Ed had a very good chance of winning.

When the dealer revealed his hand, he held seventeen points. Ed's hand won.

This was quicker than poker, and Ed felt comfortable with his level of skill. He could do this as well as poker. He settled in.

The games went well for quite some time with Ed losing some hands. Overall, he won more than he lost. His small stack of chips gradually grew larger, but time was flying away. He began to increase his bets. He won more with the good hands. He also lost more with the bad ones. He lost three hands in a row, and his small stack of chips sat lonely on the table.

It didn't take Ed long to realize Lady Luck wasn't sitting on his side here. He decided it was time to cash in and go back to the Ameristar. He had less than two hundred dollars of his original stake left. He couldn't go home now.

Unfortunately, Lady Luck deserted him at the Ameristar as well. In less than thirty minutes he lost everything.

When Ed left the casino, numbness crept over him. He's lost money before, but not like this.

He knew that if he'd used what money he had this morning, he could have paid a good portion of his debt. He'd been so sure he would win eventually. In fact, he was still sure he could do it. All he needed was another stake.

Luck came in spurts—both good and bad. He'd had his bad spurt, so now it was time for a winning streak to come by again.

The more Ed thought about it, the more he was sure things would turn around, if he could just get to the tables. Where could he get another stake? He had to find the money and get to the casino. He refused to go home busted.

He thought about calling LaMont for a loan. He dismissed that idea almost as soon as it came to him. His brother would be next to impossible to locate on such short notice, and besides, his money was all tied up in school expenses. On top of that, LaMont could be unbelievably snoopy when he set his mind to it.

There was no way Ed could go to anyone at church, or even at work, for a loan.

He pulled out the checkbook and studied the balance. Two hundred and fifty dollars, and every penny spoken for. His family needed groceries, the electric bill was due, and the gas bill, too. He needed gasoline to get to and from work. It would take every last dime to carry them until his next payday.

Still, if he took that money, or just two hundred dollars of it, and could win a few hands of poker, they could pay those bills and get some of the others off their back, too.

Ed drove to the bank.

In less than an hour he entered the casino garage again and parked. Ten minutes later he sat at a poker table, a stack of chips sitting by his hand. He could win this time. He could feel Lady Luck sitting on his shoulder. He knew some of the players at this table, and he knew their tells. This would be his lucky session.

Chapter 26

$\mathcal{I}$t surprised Ed to see it was dark when he rolled out to the van. Kathy and Zoe would be worried about him. Time had slipped by so quickly, and with no clock in the casino and the daylight-bright sky painted on the ceilings, who could tell it was late?

For Ed it was way too late, not only in time, but in circumstances. How would he tell Kathy he'd lost all their money? What would he use to buy gas the next week? He couldn't even use Kathy's more economical car, because it didn't have the special controls he had to have to drive.

Even more pressing was where they would get grocery money.

Ed couldn't believe how unlucky he'd been over and over. Nobody lost all the time, not even him. He'd won a few hands, and he realized now it was just enough to keep him playing. Lady Luck flirted with him and teased him. In the end she sat with a different player.

Ed wiped the perspiration from his brow and tried to think. He couldn't go home and tell Kathy they couldn't eat this week. He just couldn't.

LaMont should be home by now, or his roomies should be able to find him. Ed drove to North Kansas City and hunted for a pay phone. Everyone else in the world owned a cell phone, but he couldn't afford one. Someday, he promised himself, someday he and Kathy would have all those sorts of things.

Right now he needed a phone. Finally he found one. His first call was to Kathy. "I'm sorry, honey. I've run into a little trouble. I should be home in a couple of hours."

"What sort of trouble?" Kathy asked, her voice full of fear.

"Don't worry. Nothing I can't handle," Ed said. "I gotta go right now. I have to make another call. See you in a couple of hours. Bye."

He hung up before Kathy got beyond her protesting, "But—"

He didn't know how to explain this mess to her, and if he could reach LaMont and borrow a few bucks, he wouldn't have to.

"What'cha mean you need two hundred and fifty dollars?" LaMont asked. "You make a lot more money than I do, Bro."

"I know," Ed agreed. "I've had a couple of reverses. I'll pay you back when I get paid next week, I promise."

"What kind of reverses?" LaMont pushed. "You in some sort of trouble, man?"

"Naw." Ed didn't want LaMont to know how stupid he'd been. He should have quit the tables when he started to lose. There was always another day. He'd let his emotions get in the way of his judgment. The few hands he'd won had given him a rush of confidence that his luck was back. He should have waited for a better day.

"I'm just short this week," he told his brother. "We need groceries and gas money until I get paid. That's all."

Ed held his breath, and worry pounded him during the long silence on the phone. "I'm good for it. You know me," he told his brother.

"Yeah," LaMont said "I've got the money right now. Trouble is I'm close to being strapped myself. In two weeks I need a bunch of books and I have some other bills, too. I gotta have the money by then."

"You will," Ed promised. "I won't let you down."

It took thirty minutes to get to the dorms and pick up the cash. "You want to go out to the house and eat?" he asked.

LaMont glanced at his watch. "You not eat yet? Kathy's gonna skin you, man. It's eight o'clock. Ain't no way I'm goin' in for supper now."

Ed groaned. LaMont was right. It was later than he'd thought. Kathy would be more than a little worried. She'd be livid.

All Ed could hope for was some sort of damage control. He didn't want anything to come between him and Kathy. They had too much good between them to lose it now.

He tried to decide, as he drove home, what to say to her, and it wasn't easy. It wouldn't have been all that hard if he'd won, but he'd lost. Now things were all messed up.

He wanted—no, he needed—to pray, just like Micah had taught him to do in times of trouble, but how did he face God now? There was really no point. He didn't even know how to face Kathy, let alone his Creator.

At home, Zoe greeted him at the door, Desmond in her arms. "Kathy's waiting for you," she said without preamble.

"I know." Ed couldn't meet her questioning gaze. "I'll go now," he said, eager to escape the questions he was sure she wanted to ask.

"I'm sorry," he said, the moment he entered their bedroom. "I should have called earlier, but my watch is broken."

Kathy sat propped against the headboard, and her eyes snapped with anger. "You couldn't see it was getting dark? You don't know what time the sun goes down?"

"I'm really sorry, Kathy," he said again.

"Where were you? You smell like smoke." Her jaw jutted, and he knew she wouldn't let this go. Not his Kathy who never tackled anything halfheartedly.

He sighed and rolled his chair close to her side of the bed. He reached for her hand and tried to swallow his self-disgust.

"I went to the casinos," he said, "and none of them have clocks. I guess they don't want me to know what time it is," he said lamely.

Kathy studied him for a long moment, and he could feel her disappointment. He was sure she could tell he'd lost. Kathy knew him, and could read him better than any human on earth. She didn't need him to say another word.

"How much?" she asked.

He squirmed in his chair. He didn't want to lie to Kathy, but he didn't want to tell her about the other trips he'd made before today.

"More than we can spare," he said.

Her eyes grew cold. She might as well have slapped him. "How much more?"

He knew it wouldn't help to hedge. "Two hundred and fifty dollars. That's why I'm this late," he rushed on. "I called LaMont and borrowed the money. We'll be okay until I get paid."

"We're not okay," she said. "If you repay LaMont then, where will you get the money for the bills due that pay period?"

Ed watched his hands as he clasped and unclasped them, then ran them across his thighs in an effort to relax them. "I don't know," he said.

Kathy searched his face and asked, "Why, Ed? You promised you wouldn't gamble any more."

He shook his head. "I didn't break a promise to you, Kathy. I didn't!"

He tried to pick up her hand, but she shoved it beneath the sheet. "I told you I wouldn't gamble online any more, and I didn't. I haven't gambled on another casino site since I made that promise to you."

Kathy's voice quavered. "Ed, how could you do this?"

He sat silent, his head lowered, for so long she demanded, "Well?"

He looked up into her angry eyes and pleaded for her understanding. "I was trying to help, Kathy. I wanted to get us out from under this day-to-day horror. We're not living; we're existing."

Kathy didn't let up. "And losing what little money we had is helping? I don't see how."

"I know," Ed agreed, "but if I had won, we'd be okay now."

Kathy shook her head, and her voice sounded sharp. "You know better than that, Ed. You can't beat the casinos." She sounded more sad than angry now.

Ed couldn't stand her pity, or her disappointment. "But I can, Kathy. I have. I went there today with two thousand dollars I'd already won. It is possible to win."

The moment the words left his mouth, he knew he'd made his worst mistake of the day.

"You left home with two thousand dollars this morning, and now you're telling me you lost all of that plus two hundred and fifty dollars we needed for bills?"

"I know it sounds bad." He leaned closer. "But if I'd won, like I planned, we'd be able to pay everything off before the baby came. Don't you see? It's the only way I know how to get ahead."

"And don't you see?" Kathy snapped, "We are not ahead. We are two hundred and fifty dollars deeper in debt."

Ed nodded. "Yes, but I won before, and I can do it again. I just had a bad day. Luck goes around and comes around, but skill plays into poker, too. I know how to play. I just needed to stay away from the blackjack tables. I won't make that mistake again."

"No," his wife agreed harshly. "You won't, because if you do, I will leave you, Ed Johnson. I will not live with a compulsive gambler."

He sank low into his chair, too shocked for words. She couldn't mean that. They both knew what the Scriptures said about divorce. He had never looked at another woman, let alone touched one. Kathy was the one woman he loved, and he couldn't even begin to think of life without her by his side. "You don't mean that," he said.

As though she read his thoughts, she said, "I won't divorce you, Ed. I know the Scriptures just like you do, but I don't have to live with you." She paused for emphasis, glaring at him. "I will not live with a man who purposely keeps me on the edge of a financial cliff, ready to jump and pull me off, too."

He nearly gagged on the anger that boiled up from his belly all the way into his throat. "Okay, so how do you suggest I help our finances? I can't find a part-time job, and I couldn't get everyone where they need to be, even when I did find one. What do you expect me to do?"

"I don't know," Kathy hissed, "but not that." She glared long enough for him to look away before she repeated softly, "Not that."

Chapter 27

*E*d spent the night on the sofa, which was somewhat awkward with Zoe in the house. He told her there was a late show on TV he wanted to watch. Zoe was down for the night long before he shifted himself from his chair to the sofa and tried to sleep.

He dozed off and on, but most of the night he replayed the day's events over and over.

What could he have done differently at the casinos to make things turn out better? He knew he should have quit when he lost that first five hundred dollars at the Ameristar. He should have waited for another day, but he'd wanted to bring enough money to Kathy to pay all their debts.

He'd been greedy. If he hadn't been so impatient, he could have won. He knew it. On top of that, those two old ladies had worked him, and the rest of the players at their table, too. He should have seen that coming, but who would expect a couple of polished blue-hairs to be hustlers?

One thing for certain, he'd learned a lesson or two. Next time he wouldn't let greed get to him, and he'd watch the amateurs.

He thought about Kathy's threat, too. He knew she'd been upset, or else why was he here on the sofa? He also knew she could be stubborn, but he was secure in her love, and when she had time to think about it, and realized he was trying to help them out of this financial pit, he thought she would relent. Kathy loved him, but she was stubborn. She wouldn't want to, but if she said she would leave, she'd do it, unless he could reason with her.

Still, he didn't want her upset again. That kind of turmoil couldn't be good for her or the baby. In the future, he had to be certain she didn't find out about his trips to the casino.

He knew his luck wouldn't be bad forever. He just needed to wait a couple of weeks and let Kathy calm down, and let his luck come back around. Once he won and got things back on track, Kathy would have to understand. He didn't believe for a minute that she would leave him, if he could make her understand, but he didn't want to harm her or his child either.

The next day Ed bought groceries and gasoline and took what was left of LaMont's money and paid some of the most pressing bills. He often wanted to pray, but how could he expect God to hear him after the way he'd messed things up?

He ran his thoughts over and over, like a tape recorder replaying them.

I can win again.

I shouldn't go back to the casinos.

Kathy would get over it, especially when I win.

What would I do if she did leave me?

Where is God? Why doesn't he do something?

What else can I do to get the bills under control?

Each time Ed allowed his thoughts to fly down this path he grew angry. Kathy was bedfast, and the only option Ed could see was to visit the casinos again. He would just have to play smarter and be more careful.

Kathy prayed harder than she had in years. Ed was slipping onto sinful ground. He'd been there before, and her right along with him, before they both became Christians. She remembered how that all changed when Micah baptized them.

They'd both been washed clean, and they'd made a lifetime commitment to serving God and doing his will. Now Ed was straying. Kathy knew how frustrated Ed must feel over the bills. She felt it, too, but given time they could handle it all. She told herself again, they just needed to tuck their heads down and work harder.

God, help Ed to see we can do this with your help. He's impatient because he's trying to protect me, and I know that, but he has to stop gambling. Help him find his way back to you.

Even after that prayer, Kathy decided she needed to call in extra troops. She picked up the phone and dialed the church.

"Hi, Lacey. Is Micah available?"

Kathy smiled at Lacey's cheerful voice. Even if she didn't get the help she needed, just hearing Lacey's chipper tone made things seem easier to bear.

"Hold on a sec, Kathy. He's out in the hall with LaMont, trying to mount a new bulletin board on the wall."

Kathy didn't want to be a bother. Her problem didn't crop up in an instant, and waiting a few minutes wouldn't be a problem.

"This isn't that urgent, Lacey. Why don't you just have him call me when they finish?"

"Will do," Lacey said before she added, "Are you okay? You sound a little stressed."

Kathy appreciated Lacey's concern. She wasn't ready to confide in her, at least not yet. "I'm battling pregnancy blues," she said truthfully, "but your Aunt Zoe is keeping me straight. I just need to talk to Micah a few minutes and let him talk me into a better mood. He has a way of wrapping Scripture right around my heart."

Lacey chuckled. "He does at that—not just for you, but for a lot of folks. Hold on a sec. He just walked back into the office. I'll put you on hold, and he'll pick up in his office."

"Thanks, Lacey."

When Micah picked up the phone, Kathy had to exert all her will to keep from crying. "Micah, can you come by my house some time today? I need to talk to you about Ed, and I need you to pray for us."

Micah's caring voice washed over her. "I have a meeting at ten this morning, but I can cancel it if you need me now, or Margaret and I could come by this afternoon around one."

Kathy didn't want to interrupt Micah's meeting. She hated to ask him to come at all, but she needed someone to help her decide what to do. She couldn't stand the thought of leaving Ed. She loved her husband so much she ached with it. She knew he was caught up in a vortex spiraling to financial and spiritual destruction, and if it took leaving Ed to get his attention, she would. She hoped Micah might be able to offer a better suggestion.

"This afternoon is fine, Micah. I just need to talk to you and the doctors don't want me out of bed, especially this close to my due date."

"I'll see you around one. Is there anything I can do in the meantime?"

Kathy loved Micah for his concern. "You can pray for wisdom for me, and for Ed. We have some decisions to make, and I need your input, and I need God's help, too."

"I can do that," Micah assured her before he hung up.

Kathy continued to pray. The only time she stopped talking to God was when Zoe or Desmond entered the room.

Zoe brought a lunch tray and set it across Kathy's lap. "Now, you eat up, young lady," she said before she handed Kathy a napkin.

"Not to worry," Kathy said through a broad smile. "I love these open-faced sandwiches you make. What is this one?"

"Chicken and grape salad." Zoe adjusted the tray, then stood back and watched Kathy's reaction.

"Yum," Kathy glanced down at Desmond and giggled. "I see Desmond likes it, too."

Zoe looked at the toddler and shrugged. "What could I do? He screamed when he saw me pick up your tray. I did take time to wipe his hands, and I tried to clean his face, but he seems to have dodged most of my efforts."

Kathy eyed the trace of salad dressing that spread across one of Desmond's cheeks. "It sort of looks like a map of Australia."

"Well, as soon as I can catch him that mess will definitely be down under," Zoe said with a chuckle.

"Good," Kathy said. "Just for your information, Micah and Margaret will be here in a few minutes. I need to discuss some things with him."

Zoe studied Kathy a moment. "That sounds heavy. Maybe Desmond and I need to go to Penguin Park for an hour or two."

Kathy raised her eyebrows in surprise. "How do you always know exactly what to do at exactly the right moment? You are amazing."

Zoe shrugged. "I don't know. Lots of practice, maybe?"

She smiled and turned in an effort to take Desmond's hand before he shrieked and ran into the hall. The sound of his giggles trailed him back to the kitchen.

Zoe smiled, lifted her hands in exasperation, and went to follow him. "He wants more. I might as well wait and clean it all at the same time."

"Oh, Zoe, you are so good with him. What am I going to do when you go home?"

Zoe stopped, shook a finger at Kathy and said, "You stop that worrying right now, missy. I'm not going anywhere until after you have that baby, and then you can take care of both your children yourself. So just brace up and get ready. You're going to need all that energy you can store, and then some."

Chapter 28

When Micah and Margaret arrived, Kathy didn't waste any time with preliminaries. "Micah, Ed is gambling. He has been for quite a while. That's how he got my car and retrofitted the van."

Margaret sucked in a deep breath and said, "I think I should wait in the living room." She patted Kathy's hand and said, "If you need me, just call."

Kathy nodded as she struggled to stifle her tears.

Micah sat by Kathy's bed, and she gulped down the lump in her throat when she saw the sadness wash across his face. She wished Ed could have seen it, too, because that alone might have been enough to stop him.

"I was afraid it was something like that," Micah said. "I knew when he asked for the congregational prayers he must have done something he considered pretty serious."

Kathy bit her lip. "Unfortunately, I'm the one who thought it was serious. If I hadn't made such a fuss, I'm not sure he would have asked at all."

Micah nodded. "I see. I take it he didn't stop, then?"

Kathy grabbed a tissue and wiped her leaky eyes. "I think he did for a little while. He had been gambling online and he promised me he wouldn't do that any more."

"But he broke his promise?" Micah asked.

"Not technically." Kathy studied her hands and fingered the edges of the sheet. "He didn't gamble online. Now he has the van and can drive, so he went to the riverboats."

"Oh, my." Micah sighed before he asked. "How bad is it?"

Kathy's shame smothered her words to a mere whisper. "He's lost over twenty-two hundred dollars."

Micah's eyes grew huge in shock. "I didn't know he had that kind of money. I thought you two were seriously struggling to meet your monthly bills."

"We are," Kathy cried. "That's what makes this so terrible." She explained how Ed had lost not only the two-thousand dollars he'd previously won, but Lamont's two hundred and fifty dollars as well.

"If it wasn't for LaMont, he wouldn't even have gas money to get to work, or groceries for this week—and after we pay LaMont back, I don't know what we'll do for next week."

Micah sat a moment, apparently trying to absorb all Kathy had told him. Finally he spoke. "Well, at least it isn't any worse than a few hundred dollars. He could have lost the house and your cars, too."

Kathy found it hard to contemplate the degree of loss Micah described. She and Ed were already in far deeper trouble than she could imagine. In fact, she didn't know what to do as it was.

"I need some suggestions," she told Micah. "The baby is due soon, and we have no money to pay even the adjusted hospital bill. We need to pay LaMont his money so he can buy his books. When we do that I don't know how we'll eat next week. I guess you're right. Things could get worse. I don't know what I would do if it does. I don't seem to be able to handle the situation as it is. I've prayed 'til I'm purple, and I still need answers."

Micah took her hands. "Kathy, we all have times when it seems God isn't listening to us, but he does hear us. Sometimes people have to reach a point of being ready to accept God's answers. It doesn't sound like Ed was ready to listen. From what you've told me, he still may not be receptive. Have you talked with him about this?"

Kathy shook her head. "Not as much as we need to. He doesn't seem to want to hear what I have to say. He keeps telling me the Bible says a man who doesn't provide for his family is worse than an infidel. He seems to have some warped idea that gambling is taking care of us."

A tiny smile crept over Micah's mouth. "I can see Ed reasoning like that, especially since he won enough to fix the transportation problem. It appears his motive is good, Kathy. It's his method that is faulty. Do you think he'd let me to talk to him about this?"

Her tears ran more freely now, for Kathy hated having "tattled" on Ed, but she needed Micah's help before things got any worse. "He'll be angry when he finds out I've talked to you, but I think he'll listen. I'd rather we starve to death than have Ed lose his soul."

Micah patted Kathy's hands. "I don't think it will come to that. We have the food pantry at church, and when needed, we have some funds to help people through hard times. I thought you knew that, Kathy."

She glanced up and wailed, "I thought that stuff was for destitute travelers, and people who have house fires and things like that."

Micah chuckled. "They are." He patted her hand. "They're also for people like you and Ed who need a little boost. It doesn't sound like you're going to need a lot. After the baby comes, I assume you'll go back to work?"

"I can go back to the investment company," Kathy wiped her eyes again, "but I'll have to find another evening job, if Zoe agrees to stay on and keep the babies in the evening."

Micah frowned. "I don't know, Kathy. Zoe isn't a young woman any longer. It might be too much for her to take on both children."

"Maybe," Kathy agreed, "and Ed doesn't want me to work evenings. We have to do something."

"Let me think about it," Micah said as he leaned back in his chair. "In the meantime, I'll talk to Ed and see if we can get him curbed from the gambling."

"He isn't going to like that," Kathy said, 'but I think he'll respect what you have to say."

"Nobody likes 'reproof and correction,' Kathy, but that's part of my job. I'm supposed to keep men's souls safe, and gambling means Ed's walking in an oil slick. It's just a matter of time before he falls away from his faith completely, if we don't turn him around."

Kathy knotted the edge of the sheet in her fist. She didn't want to think of Ed falling, but she knew Micah was right. "When can you meet with him?"

"The sooner the better," Micah said. "Will he be home tonight?"

Kathy wasn't sure. Ed had gone to his "other job" frequently. Suddenly her eyes flared. "I don't know, Micah. He works late a lot, and he told me he had an evening job. Now I think he must have been going to the boats all those evenings."

Micah thought a moment. "Then maybe you should call me when he gets home, or do you think I should ring him at work and make an appointment to talk to him?"

Kathy wasn't sure. "Maybe you should contact him. I'm afraid he'll go back to the casinos and not come home until late."

Micah rose from his chair. "I'll call as soon as Margaret and I get back to the office. In the meantime, you quit worrying. I'll talk to the elders and the deacon in charge of benevolence, and we'll get you some groceries. I'll wait until Sunday afternoon before I fill Ed's gas tank so he'll be able to get to work next week. You're going to be fine," he assured.

Chapter 29

*E*d clinched his jaw. He couldn't believe Kathy had talked to Micah about their money problems, and if that wasn't enough, she'd ratted him out, too.

"I don't have a gambling problem," he insisted. "I've never had one. I'm just trying to get me and Kathy out of debt."

Micah listened as Ed ranted.

"Why'd Kathy pull you into this anyway?"

Micah sank into his office chair and motioned Ed into position opposite his desk. "Ed, Kathy tells me you recently lost over twenty-two hundred dollars. In your present financial state, I'd say that is a problem."

Ed couldn't deny what Micah said. "Yeah, that was a problem, but it was just one day. I'll win next time, and then Kathy and me can pay our debts, and I can quit. The Bible says a man who doesn't provide for his own is worse than an infidel."

Micah shook his head. "Listen to yourself, Ed. It is important to care for your family, but God has never condoned hurting others to do that. If you're patient, you can overcome your bills with your job."

"Not before we pile up more with this new baby," Ed snapped. "How am I going to pay that bill, let alone all mine that I already have?"

Micah's soft tone irritated Ed. He wanted to fight this out, and Micah was much too calm. "I been praying," Ed sulked, "and it didn't do no good. If I hadn't done something about the car, I'd be out of a job by now."

Again, Micah shook his head. "No, Ed. Bruce and I were working on that, and we almost had the rides worked out for you. We quit trying when you showed up with the van retrofitted."

Ed stared at Micah a long moment. "What did you have going?" he asked in disbelief.

"Bruce knew about a used mini-van the school district was selling. It needed some work, but we thought Brother Kilgore could fix it in his garage."

Ed sat and glared out the window for a long moment. "It's not like I can't quit," he finally said.

"Then prove it," Micah challenged. "Quit before you lose even more. If you're as broke as Kathy says, there isn't anything left to wager without jeopardizing things you need to survive."

Ed leaned forward for emphasis. "But I can win, Micah. I've won before, and I can win again."

"Maybe," Micah agreed, "and where does that leave the people you play against?"

"That doesn't matter," Ed said, eager to make his point. "Everybody knows they'll lose some."

"You don't seem to think you will," Micah countered.

Ed smacked the desk top. "Yes, I do. I know everybody loses some. The idea is to control your losses."

Micah still refused to buy into Ed's argument. "So what happened to you last week? The story Kathy told didn't sound like there was much control exerted that day."

"Okay," Ed agreed. "I let it get out of hand. I won't do that again. I'll pull out before it gets that bad."

"Again," Micah said, "what about those who lose? Many play long enough to lose their homes and their businesses."

Ed couldn't believe Micah was so obtuse. "That's not my fault, or my problem."

"I maintain it is." Micah's tone was gentle but firm. "If you're sitting at that table, you are part and parcel of the game. You are just as morally responsible as an accomplice in a bank robbery."

Ed blinked and opened his mouth to protest, then snapped it shut again. He hadn't thought about his gambling in that light. In prison he'd met more than one man who'd been convicted as an accomplice to one crime or another. Was Micah right? He wanted to shout "No," but he wasn't sure.

"Even if it's true that you can stop whenever you want," Micah pushed, "what about the other players who can't and don't? What sort of influence are you when you're sitting in a seat at the same table with them? You know the Scripture says to abstain from even the appearance of evil. Even if it is something that is not actually wrong, but it might cause someone else a spiritual problem, we're told not to do those things. In view of that, my question to you is this: Is going to a casino abstaining from the appearance of evil?"

Ed slowly bowed his head, unable to meet Micah's gaze any longer. "No," Ed agreed. "No, it isn't." He sat and stared at his hands and tried to swallow the egg called an Adam's apple. "Micah, I didn't mean to hurt anyone. I just want to get my life in order and be able to give Kathy and Desmond and our new baby the things they need."

"I know, Ed." Micah leaned forward and laid one of his hands over Ed's on the edge of the desk. "You've grown so much in your Christianity. I've been proud to see how you've matured, and it hurts me for you to have slipped in this area. The good news is that you can fix it."

Ed glanced up, not sure what Micah expected of him. "How?"

Micah leaned back and held Ed's gaze. "By repenting, and praying, and then making sure it doesn't happen again."

Ed just couldn't see what Micah wanted now. He'd already gone before the congregation and asked for their prayers. "I've already done all that," he said flatly.

Micah studied him long enough that Ed wanted to whirl his chair and leave.

"Have you?" Micah asked. "You asked for our prayers, but did you really repent, Ed? It's not my job to judge you, but it is important to me that you understand what the problem is, and that you have your soul right with God."

That did it! Ed could defend himself from now until time ended, but when Micah pulled his ace and told Ed how much he cared about how he conducted himself, Ed just couldn't bring himself to disappoint him any longer. If Micah was unhappy, how must God be feeling?

Micah went on. "You do understand what all repentance involves, don't you?"

Ed sighed, then nodded. "Yes. I know I need to be sorry for my sin." He paused.

"And?" Micah prodded.

"And I need to decide not to let it happen again." Ed sank back deeper into his chair.

"That's right," Micah agreed. "It is a complete change of direction as well as a change of heart."

Ed understood, and he'd known all this when he first asked for prayers, but he hadn't been ready to change what he was doing. He still wasn't sure he could let the gambling go. He and Kathy needed the money he knew he could win if he just kept his cool.

Micah must have understood his turmoil, or maybe he just got worried because Ed sat silent so long. He went on. "Ed, God has promised we won't go without the things we need. He did not promise we'll have everything we want. If it is something we really need, we'll get it. If you believe God has a place prepared for you in heaven, why is it so hard to believe this?"

Ed shrugged. "I guess because I think it is up to me to do this."

Micah nodded. "It is up to you to do all you are able, within the range of right things. Then you need to be still and let God do his thing. As the song says, "It might surprise you what the Lord can do."

Ed looked up and let a thin smile escape. "That's hard, Micah. It's really hard for me to do."

Micah actually laughed aloud. "And you think it isn't hard for anyone else?"

Irritation washed over Ed. "It doesn't look so hard for other people from where I'm sitting."

"Oh, Ed," Micah said through a sigh. "If you only knew how many people struggle with problems just like yours, and a lot of them make mistakes along the way, just like you. The difference in them and you is I know you have a good heart, and you want to please God. That's why I knew if I talked to you about this, you would do what's right."

Ed grimaced. "So what is right, Micah? How do I make sure I don't slip up again and go back to the casinos?"

Micah sorted through some loose papers on his desk, then extended one to Ed. "If you're sure you're ready to quit, there is a phone number here for the Missouri Bets Off hotline. You can call and place yourself on their master list. After that not a casino in the state will allow you to gamble in their facility."

Ed's head jerked up. "You're kidding! They have a list like that?"

"Yes, they do," Micah said. "The list goes to all the computers in every casino in the state, and they won't let you buy chips again."

Ed considered that. He should be able to quit on his own. If he put his name on the list, he would never be able to gamble in Missouri again. What if he wanted to just go play a friendly little game sometime? He wouldn't be able to.

"I don't know . . . I can quit without doing that." He didn't look at Micah. He didn't want the preacher looking deep into his soul.

Micah didn't pull back even a little bit. "Maybe you can, Ed, but I can see by your hesitation it's still a temptation for you. Do you really want to have to make this decision over and over? If you decide now to sign up, you won't have to struggle with it any longer. You will have already made the better choice."

Ed pushed himself deep into his chair and straightened his full height. "I know you're right. I just have a hard time trusting God to take care of all our financial needs."

Micah grinned. "You're not the only one. I think most of the men ever born have to face that issue many times in their lifetime."

"Then I guess I'm in good company," Ed said. He looked down at the paper Micah had given him. "This is an eight-hundred number. I can call from home."

Micah again studied Ed a moment before he said, "You could call from here right now, if you wanted to."

Ed's face flushed so quickly he suddenly needed some air. Didn't Micah trust him? He'd said he would quit going to the casinos. He'd even admitted his fears about his own and his family's future. Wasn't that enough?

"I need to get home. Kathy will be worried about me," he said, refusing to meet Micah's gaze any longer. He turned his chair and headed toward the door.

Micah rose, and followed him. "Ed, if you feel I'm pushing you, I'm truly sorry, but this is important, not only for your soul's sake but also for your relationship with Kathy. If the trust between marriage partners is destroyed, it usually strains the relationship to the point of a breakup. I love you and Kathy too much to stand by and let that happen. I'll do everything I can to stop it."

Ed knew Micah's words were true, and problems with Kathy were the last thing he needed or wanted. He also knew that if he hadn't already destroyed Kathy's trust in him, he certainly had dented it deeply.

"I'm working on all this, Micah, and I know your intent is for the good. I promise to be more patient and give God time to work his plans, if you promise to keep praying for us."

"That's easy enough," Micah said as he swung the door open for Ed. "I always pray for you and Kathy." He suddenly held up his hand to halt Ed's exit. "Wait a minute. I almost forgot. I have something for you."

Ed watched his friend rush back to his desk and open the top drawer. When he returned, he extended his hand with a check in it.

"This is to help you and Kathy through next week when you have to pay LaMont what you borrowed. If you go cash the check today, you can repay him tonight at Bible study. That will leave your work check intact to take care of your own needs."

Ed shook his head even as he stared at the amount on the check. It was enough to pay LaMont and then some. "I can't take that, Micah. You and Margaret can't afford to do this. I know Quinthia's been in the hospital, too."

"You take it," Micah insisted as he pressed the check closer. "This isn't my money. It's from the church, and don't you go getting all puffy and proud on me. We set this fund up to help people who need it. You and I both know that right now you and Kathy need this. When you get back on your feet, you can do your part to keep this fund healthy for someone else."

Ed swallowed the lump in his throat, or at least he tried to. It didn't seem to want to go away. "I've never been around people like you before. Every time I think you and the church are the greatest people on earth, you go and do something that makes me think even more of you."

Micah's chuckle startled Ed. "You just got detoured a little. You already have most of the Christian traits down pat."

The two men moved down the hall toward the main entrance. Micah continued. "That's what following the Bible does to you. It helps Christians act like Christ. When we do that, we are the greatest people on earth," Micah added before he pushed the heavy glass door open for Ed. "That includes you, when you follow the pattern."

All the way home Ed thought about all Micah had said. He stopped at the bank to deposit the check, relieved his family could eat the following week. He knew all Micah said was true. The gambling had to stop, and he had to rely on God more. What kind of faith was it if he didn't believe the promises in the Bible? A snippet of Scripture popped into his mind. "Faith comes by hearing . . ."

Ed had gone to church regularly, but he had to admit his mind often wandered into money worries rather than focusing on the sermons, and he'd almost quit reading his Bible. Was that his problem? He wasn't feeding his faith with God's word. Was he spiritually starving himself to death? He knew he was. He rationalized he hadn't had time to read like he knew he should. How could he read when he was so busy trying to make a living?

He stopped at a red light, and while he sat waiting for it to change, it occurred to him all his struggles to resolve his money issues had been in vain. He acknowledged he would have been better off to sit quietly and read and absorb God's word. Sitting in the casinos every evening hadn't helped anything.

Ed wadded the paper with the Bets Off number into a tiny ball. He didn't need to call the number and let someone else police him. He knew what he needed to do to please God, and he intended to do it. His casino visits were now a thing of the past.

Chapter 30

*W*hen Ed got home, Zoe stood at the front window watching for him. The moment he stopped, she jerked the front door open. "Kathy needs you. I think she's in labor."

Ed didn't even speak. Instead he wheeled to their room as quickly as he was able. "Kathy, are you okay?"

His wife sat on the edge of the bed, panting. Ed immediately recognized the signs of a hard contraction.

"How far apart?" he asked as he rolled to her side and took her hand. She squeezed so hard he thought she might break some of his bones, but he didn't pull back.

Finally the contraction passed, and she replied, "Five minutes. We need to call the doctor, and my suitcase is packed."

"It's ready and waiting," Zoe said from the doorway. "Desmond is in bed, so I'll stay here. Ed, you be sure to call me as soon as this baby arrives."

"I promise." Ed headed toward the phone. "Can you help Kathy get her shoes on and walk her to the van while I call the doctor and get her suitcase loaded?"

"I surely can." Zoe went to find Kathy's shoes.

Second babies usually came quicker than the first, but Ed didn't expect to hold his new daughter just an hour and forty-five minutes after they arrived at the hospital.

Pride swelled his chest so tight he found it near impossible to speak. Even with that huge lump in his throat he couldn't hold back the words. "She looks like you, Kathy. Look at that high forehead and that little pointy nose. It's not flat like mine. She's a keeper," he rushed on.

Kathy took her soft, latte-brown daughter and opened the blanket. She counted short stubby toes and long, slender, perfectly formed fingers.

Ed watched Kathy cuddle and coo to their daughter, and he shot up a short prayer of thanks that they were both healthy and safe, then said, "We've been so busy we haven't decided on a name. What do you want to call her?"

"I've been thinking about that." Kathy held the baby so both she and Ed could see the little girl. "I thought about another name with a "D" to go with Desmond, but I couldn't think of anything I liked. I want something special for our little girl."

Ed ran a list of names through his mind, but they all seemed ordinary.

The silence grew long in the room, save the soft suckling noises the baby made as she nursed at her fist.

Ed studied the tiny form. "She's hungry."

Kathy smiled. "She's always hungry. I just fed her thirty minutes ago."

"Then she needs a pacifier." Ed searched the bedside table and handed over a pink Binky to Kathy, who popped it into the baby's mouth.

"What about Shalinda?" she asked.

Ed frowned. "It's different, but it doesn't seem to fit her. How about Charis?"

"I like it." Kathy moved the baby to her other arm. "But where did you get that name?"

Ed shrugged. "I don't know. I just heard it sometime, and I liked it. It sounds classy."

"I like it, too." She shifted their daughter to rest on her legs so both she and Ed could talk to her. "Hello, Miss Charis. Welcome to our family."

The baby blinked, yawned wide, then closed her eyes in sleep.

"She's not impressed," Kathy said before both she and Ed burst into laughter.

"Sounds like a party in here," a deep voice said from the door.

Kathy looked up and recognized Dr. Fitzhugh. "It is a party," she told him before she added, "I'm surprised to see you here again." She noticed he wore scrubs, and a stethoscope hung around his neck.

The doctor stepped closer. "I'm doing rounds for Dr. Hughes for a few days while he takes a much-needed vacation."

Kathy's eyes flared in surprise. "He was here last night when I had my baby, and he didn't say anything about going on vacation."

Dr. Fitzhugh picked up the chart that hung on the end of Kathy's bed and glanced through it before he spoke. "That's probably because you were both a little busy, and too, I didn't convince him to actually leave until this morning. I had to promise to take very good care of all his patients."

"I'm sure you will," Ed said. "Do I need to leave?"

"Only for a couple of minutes," the doctor told him.

Ed placed Charis in the bassinette beside Kathy's bed and stepped into the hall. Dr. Fitzhugh finished his exam quickly. He chatted the whole time, which relaxed Kathy through the ordeal.

"Dr. Hughes is planning to retire soon," he said, "and I am in the process of buying his practice."

"Really?" Kathy asked in surprise. "I knew he was beginning to show some age. I guess I just expected him to carry on forever."

Dr. Fitzhugh did not look a day over thirty, if even that much. He listened to Kathy's heart, then replied. "I think he meant to, but his daughter lives in Tennessee, and she has a new baby. I think the call to be Grandpa got to be more than he could resist, especially since he lost his wife last year."

Charis began to squirm and fuss. Kathy reached over to pat the baby, certain she couldn't be hungry. "So you're moving to Kansas City?"

"Yes," Dr. Fitzhugh said as he pocketed his stethoscope. "In about six months, as soon as my house is finished."

"Oh," Kathy said, "so it will be that long before you actually take over the practice?"

"No." The doctor pulled the sheet back up over Kathy. "I'm here now. Unfortunately, my house isn't ready so I'm staying in a motel. I wish I could find a sleeping room somewhere. The noise at the motel leaves a lot to be desired, but I don't want to get locked into a long lease for an apartment, either."

"Yeah," Kathy agreed, "that is a real problem. Nobody's willing to do short-term leases. Too much work."

"Ah well, it'll only be a few months," Dr. Fitzhugh said. "In the meantime, I'm ready to send you and this cutie home."

Kathy grinned broadly. "That's great. I can't wait to see her big brother and introduce the two of them."

Ed knew he and Kathy needed to talk, but with the baby arriving and all that entailed, he hadn't had an opportunity. Truth be known, he wasn't too eager to tackle the subject. Of course, he knew he must if they were to trust one another again.

He needed to find a good time, and he didn't think having Zoe in the house would be a good thing. He decided it should be in the car. It took longer than he expected to get all Kathy's flowers from church members and co-workers loaded. The nurse helped pack Charis's things and put them on a cart. She helped Kathy and Charis into a wheelchair and then pushed them to the elevator.

Fumbling, Ed got the baby buckled into the safety seat in the back and Kathy fitted into the front, before he locked his chair down and headed home.

It was a thirty minute drive, and Ed figured it would take every bit of that to clear things up, so he started as soon as they left the parking lot.

"I was with Micah the other day when you went into labor."

Kathy stared straight ahead, apparently dreading this discussion as much as Ed did. "I know. I asked him to talk to you."

Ed gripped the steering wheel, intent on keeping this conversation civil. "You knew that would make me angry, Kathy. Why didn't you just talk to me?"

She glanced over at him, then turned back to gaze out the windshield. "I did talk to you, and you promised you wouldn't gamble online anymore. I know, you didn't do that, but you knew going to the casinos was wrong. If you hadn't thought so you wouldn't have sneaked around to do it. Since I know you knew, I figured I needed some help to make you see reason."

Ed's composure snapped. "You could have tried, Kathy. It's humiliating for Micah to know our business."

Kathy's voice rose as she slung out, "It wouldn't be if you weren't ashamed. Do you think it won't be humiliating not to be able to pay our bills next week, because you gambled our money away? If you'd done the right thing, you wouldn't care for Micah to know all about our stuff."

Ed sucked in a breath. He had to admit what Kathy said was true. Micah knew all Ed's past crimes, Micah was the one who converted Ed and Kathy, and he knew all about Ed's being shot. In fact, Micah knew more about Ed than some of Ed's own family, because Micah had taken the time to love and care about them. Ed realized what humiliated him was the preacher discovering this new sin in his life. It hurt to see the disappointment in Micah's eyes. Ed had thought about that a lot these last two days, and it made him contemplate how disappointed God must be in him. He didn't like that feeling of being at odds with God or with Micah, and he certainly didn't want to feel that way with Kathy either.

"I know," he told his wife, "I've disappointed a lot of people. I promise you, Kathy, I won't do it again."

Kathy sat silent, her hands flexing open and shut, and Ed knew she struggled with the words. "And what loophole will you use next time, Ed? You didn't gamble online after your last promise, but you went to the casinos. This time you promise not to go back there, so will you start going to the back rooms of the corner bar?"

"No!" He shouted. "No, Kathy. I promise you I'm done with gambling."

Ed turned off North Oak onto Vivion Road before he glanced at Kathy. She sat chewing her lower lip, and he saw her thumb a tear from her eyes.

"I want to believe you, Ed. I want to trust what you say, and I want to believe what we have both worked so hard to accomplish will be safe."

"It will be," Ed assured. "I've learned my lesson, and I know it's going to be hard for me to learn to trust God to take care of us when we get in a crunch. Kathy, I'm ready to give it my all. If you and God help me, we'll make it. Okay?"

Kathy turned and flashed him a watery smile. "We will be okay, Ed. God never breaks his promises."

Ed believed that on an intellectual level. His problem was accepting it on a practical day-to-day level. He had a lot of work to do in that area, but Kathy would help him, and so would Micah.

Chapter 31

The next Sunday Ed and Kathy rose earlier than they were accustomed in order to have time to feed, bathe, and dress both Desmond and Charis. They planned to go to worship and to show off their new daughter, too. Zoe had agreed to stay the first week to give Kathy time to regain her strength. After that she said she intended to return to her own home where her new kitchen awaited.

"Won't you go with us this morning?" Kathy asked the older woman at the breakfast table. "You can help me keep up with Desmond while all the women coo over Charis."

Zoe picked up some of the breakfast dishes and headed to the dishwasher. "I guess I could go. I definitely want to be there when you show off that baby."

Kathy wished Zoe wanted to go to worship God, but if she went to show off Charis, maybe she would learn some of God's word while she was there.

By the time they arrived the service had already begun, and the little group struggled to find a pew empty enough to accommodate all five of them near the back. Kathy didn't want to sit up front in case Desmond or the baby grew too noisy and she or Ed had to leave the auditorium to quiet them. Finally an older man and woman moved to the center of the pew and made room for them.

It disappointed Kathy when Zoe spent almost the entire service fidgeting with Charis or entertaining Desmond. Kathy appreciated the help, but she'd hoped Zoe would get something from Micah's sermon. On the up side, thanks to Zoe's efforts, Kathy did manage to hear a larger chunk of the sermon than usual.

Micah spoke of love and how people should treat one another, and he spoke of trust and how easily it can be destroyed. He also talked about rebuilding damaged relationships, and how if God sent his only Son to rebuild his relationship to man, how important he must think it is to mend our personal relationships.

Kathy swallowed hard and reached out and took Ed's hand in resolve. She intended to give Ed the benefit of the doubts she had. She would trust him. She had to, both for her own emotional well being and to please God. She couldn't go through life beating Ed up at every turn. He was a good man. He'd made mistakes, but he was trying to do the right thing, and Kathy knew with God's help, and hers, he would be fine. Marriages withered under the burden of suspicion and mistrust, and Kathy had no intention of that happening between her and Ed.

Once the service ended, it took her a few minutes to gather the children's various items and repack them in the diaper bag. Well before she finished, a clutch of women surrounded them, eager to see Charis in her frilly pink lace-encrusted dress and bonnet.

"Oh, look," one woman said. "She smiled. She looks just like Kathy!"

"She didn't smile," another older woman said. "She's still asleep. That's just gas."

"Oh, Myrtle, she did too smile. Look, her eyes are open. Why, I do declare, I believe her eyes are already brown. I've never seen a baby that didn't have blue eyes when they were first born."

Another woman lifted the light blanket that covered Charis's legs. "I want to see her feet. You haven't seen a baby until you've seen her feet."

Kathy slipped the tiny soft white satin shoe and pink lace-topped sock off an even tinier baby foot.

"Me, too," a deep masculine voice chimed in.

Kathy looked up and recognized the new doctor. "Dr. Fitzhugh, what a surprise to see you here."

"Thought I was a complete heathen?" he teased. "Actually, I've been a Christian since I was twelve years old. Wouldn't miss a service if I can be here at all."

Kathy grinned at him and lifted her brows. "It's nice to see you have your priorities straight, and we're glad you chose our congregation. Welcome."

He nodded. "In addition to worship, I had to come see our girl this morning. We haven't missed seeing one another many mornings yet."

Kathy laughed. "Well, if she keeps waking up every hour and a half, I may send her to you every day."

The good doctor held out both hands in the universal stop signal. "I just deliver. I don't babysit."

Kathy finally remembered her manners and introduced him to Zoe and the other women nearby. "This is Dr. Fitzhugh."

"Jason to my friends," he said.

"Jason is taking over Dr. Hughes' practice," Kathy explained. "He'll be moving to Liberty as soon as his house is finished."

"Wonderful," Zoe exclaimed. "It will be good to have some new blood in the community. Where will you be?"

"In Whitehall addition," Jason said. "It's going to be about six months before it's finished. That's another reason I came over here. I wondered if any of you ladies knew of a vacant sleeping room I could rent for an undetermined length of time? I don't need much, since most of my time is spent at the hospital or with Dr. Hughes right now, until I learn the practice."

Myrtle spoke first. "There's the duplexes over in Place Liberty."

Jason shook his head. "I've called all the apartment complexes, and I've talked to a couple of real estate agents. Most want year-long leases, and I don't want to do that. I talked to the short-term places, and they're full right now. I'm staying in a motel, and I can go on doing that. It isn't very restful since I don't get much sleep with people coming and going all night. Nobody seems to know what quiet means in a place like that."

"Not a good situation," Zoe sympathized.

"Well, I doubt you'll find any place without a lease," Myrtle said as she slipped Charis's sock and shoe back in place.

Zoe turned to Kathy. "You have that little apartment in the basement, Kathy. Have you thought about renting it out?"

Kathy stared at Zoe in surprise. "You're kidding, right? It's so tiny you can barely turn around in it."

Jason perked up. "I don't need much room. What I need is some-place without car doors banging and people shouting right outside my window all night."

Kathy still shook her head. "You forget, doctor, we have a new baby who seems to think she needs to cry every ninety minutes."

Jason laughed. "I didn't forget," he said, "and I can't explain it, but a crying baby and slamming car doors are two different things. I guess I learned to tune out the babies as an intern. If you have a place, I'd really like to look at it."

"I don't know," Kathy said. She turned to look for Ed and Desmond, who had wandered to the vestibule. "I would have to discuss it with Ed."

Zoe took Jason's arm. "I tell you what. Why don't I take us all to lunch at the Corner Cafe, and these two can discuss it on the way there. If they decide they like the idea, you can go by the house afterward and look it over."

"But—" Kathy began.

"That's a marvelous plan," Jason interrupted, "Except I insist on buying lunch. You can consider it your finder's fee if this works out, and if it doesn't, I still get brownie points for being a nice guy."

"Done," Zoe agreed as though Kathy had no say in the matter, and in fact, it appeared she didn't.

"I'll go tell Ed," Zoe said before she slipped away.

"Well," Myrtle huffed, "she certainly took over that situation."

A tiny grin split Kathy's face. "Yes, indeed. She did, but her heart's in the right place, and how can I argue with a free lunch?"

In the car Zoe explained the proposal to Ed while Kathy sat in the back and fed Charis. Once Ed had all the details, Zoe went on, "Just think how that little bit of extra money will help out, and the basement even has its own entrance. His coming and going shouldn't disturb your lifestyle at all."

Ed shook his head. "I'm sure it's way too humble for a doctor. He won't want to live in our dinky little house."

Zoe pushed harder. "It's neat and clean. He's not looking for big and fancy, Ed. He's looking for quiet. Why don't you just let him decide? If he doesn't want it, he can say so."

Kathy saw Ed glance at her in the rearview mirror and lift his eyebrows in question.

"I don't know," Kathy said before she rummaged in the diaper bag for a dry diaper and ointment. "I seriously doubt he'd want it, but the income would be nice. We're not using that part of the house right now, except to store stuff, and that could be moved to the laundry room."

Zoe shifted in her seat so she and Kathy could see each other. "Yes, and when you close that adjoining door, you don't even have to go through there to do your laundry. I'm telling you two, this is perfect for everyone concerned."

"Maybe so." Ed stopped at a light. "But I have no clue what would be a fair price, and I'll need to fix the storm door. We've kept it locked because it sags on the hinges when it's open."

"That's simple," Zoe dismissed. "You and I can fix that this afternoon."

Ed pulled into the restaurant's parking lot and searched for a spot. He parked and turned to Kathy. "So, what do you think of this plucky little banty hen's idea?"

Kathy laughed so suddenly Desmond jumped, and Charis cried out. Kathy lifted the baby from the car seat and soothed her. "I think she's pushy, but it just might work. If you think it's a good idea, we can let him come and look. At least that will get the banty out of your face."

"Well," Zoe sputtered in mock indignation, "if this banty hadn't stepped in you would have missed this wonderful opportunity to help someone else while you help yourself." Her eyes twinkled in half jest. "I just don't see how you could have coped without me."

Ed's deep laughter combined with Kathy's giggles before Kathy said, "Okay, enough already. We'll let him decide."

Jason climbed out of his black Lexus, and Kathy's heart sank. No way would a man with that kind of taste want to live at their house. It surprised her when Jason gripped the handles of Ed's chair and pushed him inside.

They had to wait to be seated, since it was a popular establishment.

Fortunately there was room in the small waiting area for Kathy and Zoe to sit, and Jason stood.

"I can't tell you how excited I am about the prospect of getting some real sleep," he told Kathy. "If this works out, I'll be so grateful I might have to bring all of you to lunch every Sunday!"

Kathy couldn't believe this sophisticated man would be content in their humble little house, but Zoe had steamrollered them this far. Kathy couldn't see any graceful way to get out of taking Jason to the house. Before she could make any comment, the hostess called their name and seated them.

It had been a long time since Kathy had enjoyed such a meal, and she savored every bite. She could tell Ed enjoyed his equally as well.

Kathy and Zoe tended the children while Jason and Ed discussed baseball teams and players. Kathy wondered what the apartment looked like, because she hadn't been able to navigate the steps since long before Charis's birth.

"How cluttered is it down there now?" she whispered to Zoe, not sure they should take Jason home with them after all.

Zoe patted her hand. "You won't be embarrassed, Kathy. I've been dusting and vacuuming it regularly. There are some out-of-season clothes on the racks in there. We can move those today. I keep telling you, it's perfect."

After they finished their meal, Ed gave Jason the specific address and directions—"Just in case we get separated," he said.

On the way, Ed asked Zoe," So what do you think would be a fair rental fee?"

"I'm not sure," Zoe said after a moment of thought. "He's paying motel fees now. I'm sure he'd view anything less than that a bargain."

Kathy gasped. "We can't charge him anywhere close to that. He has maid service there, and I'm certainly not able to do that yet."

"Nobody says you should," Zoe told her. "I'm just saying the good doctor can afford a fair price. Certainly, don't gouge him, but don't hurt yourself either."

By the time they reached their driveway they still hadn't come up with a dollar figure.

"This is all silly anyway," Kathy said. "He isn't going to want to stay here."

Zoe took Desmond, and Kathy lifted Charis from the van, and they waited as Jason parked behind them.

Ed set the diaper bag and Kathy's purse in his lap and wheeled to the front door and unlocked it. "Come on in," he invited. "I'll let Kathy show you the apartment, since I can't roll down the steps. I could go around and meet you at the back door, but I don't think you need me."

"That's fine," Jason assured him as he glanced around. He didn't make any comment. Kathy wasn't sure whether that was due to disapproval or to male reticence to say how "cute" the place was.

She took Charis to her crib and left Desmond in Ed's care. "The stairs are over here."

At the lower stairwell, rather than Kathy turning right into the laundry room, she led Jason left into the apartment.

"It is really small," she apologized, "but it does have an apartment-sized stove and fridge, and a sink and some cabinets. The bed is only a full size, but I suppose we could store it, and you could put up a larger one if you wanted to."

Jason chuckled as he turned full circle, taking in the whole place. "I'll admit, my own bed is king-sized, but after sleeping on hard twin-sized cots all through my residency, a full-sized bed seems luxurious."

Jason started out the entry door to the yard. "Whoa. Those hinges need some attention."

"I know." Kathy held the door to keep it from flopping over. "We'll fix that today. We've just been a little busy with the baby and all."

Jason examined the door. "If you have a screwdriver, I can fix it for you. I don't think Ed could reach the top hinge."

Kathy couldn't believe a high-powered doctor had just now stood here and offered to fix her storm door.

"Well?" he asked. "Do you have a screwdriver?"

"Yes," Kathy said after she jolted herself out of her shock. "There's one in the laundry room."

"Want to get it for me?" Jason asked. His grin surprised her as much as his suggestion. She'd expected him to be thoroughly disgusted by now. She rushed to retrieve the tool and handed it to him. In a matter of seconds the door hung straight and opened and closed perfectly.

"Thanks," Kathy said when Jason handed her the screwdriver.

"My pleasure," Jason replied matter-of-factly. He went back to the kitchenette and opened the refrigerator. "This is more than perfect, Kathy. All I was looking for was a place to sleep. With this I can cook now and then, if I want to. How much are you asking for it?"

Kathy had to force her gaping mouth to behave. "You're kidding, right?"

"No, I'm not. It meets my needs perfectly. Most of my time will be spent at the hospital or in the office. When I need to sleep this will be great!"

Kathy shook her head in amazement. "Well, I never dreamed you'd want it, and we had never even considered renting it. I don't have a clue what to ask for rent."

"Well, I know what I'm paying the motel—"

"But you have maid service there. I won't be offering that." She grinned. "I have a new baby you know."

Jason's chuckle warmed her, and his response surprised her. "But this has a kitchenette the motel doesn't offer, and some peace is worth a lot, not to mention having Christians as landlords. How about we compromise?" He named a figure well beyond what Kathy imagined the apartment might be worth. Her mind all but exploded with thoughts of the bills they could trim down with this extra income.

"That sounds more than generous," Kathy said. "I do need to talk to Ed about it."

They climbed the stairs where Ed sat waiting. "So, what do you think?"

Jason walked to the front window and observed. "There's even room in the drive for my car. If you can live with my price, I'll take it."

Kathy told Ed Jason's offer, and his eyes flared in surprise. "That sounds like a lot for a studio apartment."

Jason turned and sat in the old brown chair. "It's worth it to me, especially if you'll let me move in this afternoon."

"This afternoon?" Kathy squeaked. Things were moving much too fast for her to comprehend.

"Is that a problem?" Jason asked.

"Well," Kathy began, "I need time to move those clothes out of the room, and the sheets probably need to be changed on the bed."

"I can do all that," Jason said. "I'd just like to finally get a good night's sleep."

"Wonderful," Zoe said as she pushed past Kathy. "You go get your things, and in the meantime I'll make a place in the laundry room for those clothes racks. Desmond and Kathy can take a little nap, and Ed can go to Wal-Mart and have a set of keys made for you."

Chapter 32

And that was that, Kathy thought later. It never ceased to amaze her how good God was and at times how quickly he resolved problems. This extra income, even for only a few months, should ease Ed's money worries. It would help them cope long enough for her to go back to work.

Doctor Fitzhugh moved in that afternoon, and again assured Kathy the children would not disturb him, and he insisted she should let Desmond play as loud and boisterous as he chose.

"Once I'm asleep, the only thing I respond to is my pager. The problem at the motel was getting to sleep in the first place with all the comings and goings right outside my door."

Kathy appreciated that Zoe waited until midweek, "just to be sure" Kathy was okay. Apparently assured, she insisted she needed to get back to her own home. The cabinets were done, and according to Zoe, "You and Ed need some privacy to get to know your new daughter and to help Desmond get to know her."

Kathy missed having Zoe nearby, but she also enjoyed the freedom of privacy with her family. Kathy cherished those intimate moments with the children and Ed, for she knew in six short weeks she would go back to work, and such moments would be rare.

Ed seemed to enjoy those times as well, and he was more laid back than Kathy had seen him in months. That in turn relaxed Kathy somewhat, although she did worry a lot more than she would have liked.

On the surface, Ed appeared unworried, but he still called home frequently to explain he would be working late. Kathy hated herself for her doubts. She caught herself waiting, always on edge, until Ed drove into the driveway. She knew Ed had promised he wouldn't gamble any more, but she had thought he'd made that promise before, and he'd still gone to the casinos and gambled away more money than she could imagine.

She would feel better if Ed had signed up for the Bets Off program. He'd contended he didn't need to. He'd given his word, and he insisted that was enough.

Kathy sat nursing Charis and watched Desmond play with a couple of cars on the floor nearby. She had so very much to be thankful for. The children were both healthy and perfect, Ed had a good job, as did she as soon as she recovered enough to return, and they had the extra income from the apartment to ease the medical bills. God was good, and here she sat worrying.

The thing to do was start trusting again. She needed to trust Ed to keep his word, and she needed to trust God to help him keep it. She knew what she needed to do. The problem lay in applying that knowledge.

Gradually, over the following weeks Ed set a pattern of working late two or three nights a week. Kathy strained to hide her fears from Ed, but she could not completely smother them. She couldn't seem to control the urge to talk to Bruce at church about the long hours to reassure herself that Ed truly was working and not going to the casinos. She surreptitiously watched the checking account, and she did a visual check of the pocket money Ed laid on the dresser each night before he went to bed.

It shamed Kathy to do such things, and at times it angered her that Ed's actions had pushed her to this point. Why had Ed done it? Of course, she knew why, and yet his motives were no excuse. He should have trusted God to take care of them.

And you should trust them both, her inner self chided. She decided to pray more and to try harder to trust Ed. Living with all these doubts and fears stole the joy from life, and she didn't like it. She wanted that former peace and joy they had shared when they first married. If that was to be, Kathy was the one who had to change now. Ed had already corrected his errant ways. Now Kathy needed to get hers under control.

She would force herself to refrain from calling Ed at work on his late evenings. She would quit examining the checkbook every day. She would make herself trust Ed to manage his cash well and not be a slave of fear any longer.

It took several weeks, even after Kathy went back to work, for her to be able to carry through with her resolve at least most of the time. It was harder on the nights when Ed was especially late, but she kept her fears to herself. She would overcome this.

One thing that helped was the demand from her own job. When she returned to work, many of the more difficult cases had been put on hold, awaiting her return. She was thrust into full catch-up mode.

"We didn't want to deal with these and then have you need to undo any mistakes we made," her boss told her. "We dealt with everything while you were pregnant, and I'm sure you'll have to mop up some of those cases. As soon as we knew exactly when you were coming back, we started delaying people."

Kathy eyed the stack of folders on her desk and sighed. "I don't know whether to thank you, or to kick you."

The man flashed her a grin and rubbed his chin before he replied. "Look at it this way. That pile of paper is your job security."

Kathy had to laugh at that. "Thanks, and since the job is so secure, how about a raise?" she teased.

Her boss's reply took her off guard. "We were just getting ready to call you in for a review the week you went on maternity leave. If you can carve out a half hour this afternoon at three, we can do it then."

Kathy's mouth gaped, and she quickly pulled it into control. "I was teasing."

"I know," her boss said, "but I'm serious. Three o'clock?"

"Sure," Kathy said even as the joy of anticipation swept over her. From the man's tone, she was certain she would come out of that meeting with some sort of raise.

It was several weeks later before Zoe called Kathy one evening just as she arrived home from work. Her voice sounded stressed, and Kathy strained to make sense of the call. "Lacey called . . . Micah at hospital . . . wanted you to know."

"Slow down," Kathy said as she set Charis's carrier on the floor. "Who is Micah with, and what hospital?"

"No," Zoe said. "He's not with anyone. He's in the hospital. They don't know what's wrong."

"Which hospital?" Kathy repeated.

"Liberty. They took him in an ambulance a few minutes ago. Lacey asked me to call you."

Kathy thought about where Ed would be. If he didn't work late, he'd be on his way home. She hadn't checked the answering machine yet, and she groaned when she saw the red light blink steadily. There was a message, and it was probably from Ed.

"Thanks, Zoe. I'll try to get hold of Ed, and we'll go up right away. I assume Margaret and Lacey are there?"

"Margaret is. Lacey went to get Quinthia to keep her busy until they know what's going on."

Kathy sighed in relief. That was one thing Margaret wouldn't have to worry with.

Zoe went on. "Why don't you bring Desmond and Charis here for the evening, so you can give Margaret and Micah all your attention?"

"Oh, Zoe," Kathy exclaimed, "that would be wonderful, if you're sure you don't mind." Kathy was already repacking Charis's diaper bag with formula from the fridge.

She hung up, then punched the answering machine button.

"Sorry, honey. I have a dinner with some clients tonight. It will be after that before I get home. I love you."

"Of all the times for you to be tied up late!" Kathy went to the children's room to retrieve another stash of diapers. Ed hadn't said where he was going for dinner. It was a huge city, and Bruce might have opted for one of the nice restaurants north of the river, or they might have gone to the Plaza, one of the elite dining areas of the city. It would only waste time to try to track down Ed and his party.

Kathy loaded Charis and Desmond back into her tiny red Fiesta and headed to Zoe's house.

In little more than half an hour she entered the emergency entrance of Liberty hospital. She asked for Micah at the desk.

The round, kinky-haired nurse barely glanced up. "They took him to surgery a few minutes ago. Fourth floor."

"Surgery?" Kathy asked. "What's wrong with him?"

"That's confidential," the nurse said, still studying the chart on the desk. "You'll have to ask his family. They're all up there."

Kathy turned and went to the elevators just across the hall. While she waited for the next car, she glanced at her watch. It was a little after six. From experience, she knew Ed wouldn't be home until seven-thirty or eight. Bruce liked to feed his clients well and discuss accounts at length, then turn them loose to "rest" the remainder of the evening with a full packet of information to review on their own. Kathy made a mental note to call home about a quarter after eight. Ed would want to be here with Margaret, too.

On the fourth floor Kathy followed the posted signs to the waiting room. Margaret sat alone in the tiny cubicle on one of the stiff floral-covered chairs, her eyes closed, and her lips moving with no sound. Margaret was praying.

Kathy moved quietly and slipped onto the chair beside her. The movement must have been louder than Kathy thought, for Margaret opened her eyes.

"Kathy! I'm so glad to see you. This is hard for me. I usually lean on Micah, but this time it's him who's in trouble."

"What's going on?" Kathy asked. "What happened?"

Margaret reached out and squeezed one of Kathy's hands, then held it as though letting go might allow her to float away. "He's had stomach pains almost all day, and you know how men are. I had a hard time getting him to see a doctor at all. By the time he doubled over and couldn't straighten, it was too late to get into a doctor's office, so I got him here."

"So what are they operating for?" Kathy could imagine all sorts of things, none of them good.

"He kept saying it was indigestion," Margaret said, her voice shaky, "and I knew that was a classic heart attack symptom, so I was really scared. Dr. Fitzhugh says it is his appendix, and since Micah quit hurting they think it might have burst. If it has, this could be really serious."

Kathy sank back in her chair and tried to absorb the implications of Margaret's words. "The surgeon has a good reputation. Dr. Hughes says he's tops," Kathy said, praying it was true. This was so serious Micah could die. People didn't die of an appendicitis attack in this day and age, did they? She knew it could happen, but not to Micah.

Chapter 33

$\mathcal{I}$t was eight o'clock before Kathy gave another thought to calling Ed, and when she did, there was no answer at home. She frowned and wondered where he could be. She decided maybe his dinner ran long. She knew Bruce and his crew had worked long and hard on this particular project. Maybe it took longer to present it than most of their programs. She'd try again later.

At nine-fifteen the surgeon came out and told Margaret the surgery had gone well, although the appendix had indeed burst. They cleaned the infection the best they could, and Micah was receiving a combination of high-powered antibiotics. His prognosis was good, but guarded.

"Thank you, doctor. I know Micah is in good hands, both yours and God's. He's going to be fine."

"That's what we plan," the doctor said. "You should get some rest. He won't wake enough for visitors until mid-morning."

Margaret turned to Kathy. "You go on home, Kathy. You have to work tomorrow. I'll wait until Micah is out of recovery. Then I'll go home, too."

"I don't want to leave you alone," Kathy said, certain Margaret needed her to stay.

"Nonsense." Margaret patted Kathy's hands. "You go on home. Zoe needs her rest, too, and for that matter, so does Lacey. I'll call her and let her know Micah is out of surgery, and see if she can let Quinthia spend the night. She's probably already asleep anyway."

Kathy glanced at her watch. It was almost nine-thirty. She would call Ed and have him pick up the children, and she would stay with Margaret until she was ready to leave.

Both women went to the pay phones on opposite sides of the waiting room. There was still no answer at Kathy's house, and she knew it was now time to get worried. No way would a business dinner have run this late.

Calm down, Kathy. Ed's with Bruce. Everything is fine.

She wanted to believe that, but something was definitely wrong. She decided to call Bruce's house and see if he was home.

Bruce answered on the second ring. "I don't know, Kathy. We left the restaurant about eight. He's had plenty of time to get home, I would think."

"Which restaurant?" Kathy asked, praying it was somewhere south, and the distance would account for Ed's delay. Traffic on the interstate could be murder at times.

"Our client insisted on going to the steakhouse at the Ameristar."

Kathy's heart jumped into her throat, and fear forced her heart rate into overdrive. Surely Ed hadn't gone back inside to gamble. He had no business anywhere close to that place. He should have told Bruce he couldn't go there.

Oh, Ed.

Bruce went on. "I don't like to give a casino any of my business, but this guy was adamant about the food being good, and he didn't want to go anywhere else."

Kathy hated herself, but she had to ask. "Did Ed leave when you did?"

"Yeah," Bruce said. "We all three came out together. The parking lot was nearly full when we got there, so I parked in a different lot. I didn't actually see Ed drive out."

Kathy didn't hear the rest of what Bruce said. Blood rushed into her face and ears, and her fists balled tight. Ed had promised he wouldn't gamble any more.

Maybe he didn't, she tried to console herself, *but where else would he be?* She wiped a tear from the corner of her eye.

"Thanks, Bruce."

She called Zoe. "I wanted to let you know Micah is through his surgery, and is in recovery." She explained what the doctor had said, then went on. "Are the children doing okay?"

"Of course, dear." Zoe's voice sounded cheerful. "We played some, and then I bathed them both, and now they're sound asleep. We're fine as frog's hair split four ways."

Kathy smiled at Zoe's cliché. "Would it be a problem if I leave them a little longer? I can't seem to locate Ed, and I need to go look for him."

"Of course you can, dear. What's going on?" Zoe asked, her voice full of concern.

"I'm not sure." Kathy told her friend what Bruce had said, and then added, "He may have had car problems, and he doesn't have a cell phone, so I thought I'd drive down there and see if I can locate him."

"Well, just be careful, Kathy. I don't like the idea of you being out at night by yourself, especially around the casinos."

"I'll be fine," Kathy said with more assurance than she felt. "And thanks, Zoe. I'll pick up the kids as soon as I find Ed."

"Why don't you just leave them, honey," Zoe said. "They're already asleep, and there's no need to drag them out in the middle of the night."

Kathy loved Zoe for her offer, but it wouldn't be fair. "You forget about those middle-of-the-night feedings Charis insists on."

"No, I didn't forget. We'll be fine. Now you go find Ed and get some rest. I'll see you bright and early tomorrow, and then I'll go back to bed."

"You're a peach," Kathy said before she hung up and gathered her purse.

Margaret had completed her call, and Kathy explained what the plans were. Margaret wrapped Kathy in a hug.

"He'll be fine, Kathy. He probably just had car trouble. You'll see."

"I hope that's all it is," Kathy said, still full of fear she could not share with Margaret. She didn't want anyone, not even her closest friend, to know the doubts that threatened to overwhelm her at any moment. She prayed it was merely car trouble that delayed Ed. They could deal with that. It would mean more expenses to handle, but they would somehow. If Ed was gambling, Kathy didn't know how she would ever trust him again, and where was a marriage without trust?

Her gut clenched at the thought, and she forced herself to think positive. She would find Ed safe, and he would not be at the casino. She was torn between the need to stay with Margaret and the need to find Ed. "I hate to leave you alone."

"Call me when you find him," Margaret said, "even if it's late. I'll be here awhile longer, and even if I leave, I won't rest until I know you're both safe." She gave Kathy her cell phone number, then said, "Now go on. I'm just fine."

Kathy drove by her house, but the van was not in the drive. She headed to the casino, praying all the way that she would find Ed's van broken down beside one of the streets. It occurred to her that there were several routes Ed could have chosen, so she picked the one she thought he would most likely have used.

As closely as she watched, there was no van anywhere along the way. When she turned into the long entryway to the casino, she prayed.

Please, Lord, don't let him be here. Let me find him somewhere else. Not here.

Just as she needed to make a sharp right into the casino complex, she met a flatbed wrecker, and she strained to see what he carried. "Let it be the van," she prayed. When the truck negotiated the turn, she saw it hauled a huge fancy black car. She wondered if someone had gambled it away, and the truck driver worked for a repossession company. Fear and anger crashed another roiling wave over her, and the truck's putrid odor of diesel fumes nearly gagged her.

She drove into the first lot and cruised the aisles. She didn't spot the van there, so she eased on into the parking garage. As she spiraled her way toward the top, she examined rows of vehicles on both sides of her. She reached the top tier, and was headed to the exit ramp, when she spotted the van. She looked closely, but Ed was not here.

Pure unadulterated rage nearly smothered Kathy. How could he do this? He'd made a promise to her, and she'd wanted to believe him. She'd tried hard, and she'd bitten her tongue more than once, giving him the benefit of the doubt. They were finally about to get their finances under control, and here he was jeopardizing all they had worked so hard to accomplish.

"A-r-r-r-r-g-g-g-h-h-h," she screamed her frustration in the confines of her little car. She contemplated going in and dragging Ed home.

She would if she trusted herself. She'd probably go in there and beat him half to death with her purse. Well, not really, but right now she knew she was not emotionally capable of conducting herself appropriately.

Ed, how could you? You promised!

The words rang through her mind, over and over like one of those old-fashioned cracked LP records her grandmother used to play on Sunday afternoons.

At least she knew he wasn't broken down by the side of the road, and he wasn't in some horrible wreck. Zoe was keeping the kids overnight, and it was already ten-thirty. Kathy decided to drive home and wait for Ed to show up. Maybe by the time he got home she would be composed enough to hold an intelligent conversation.

No, she decided as she drove up North Chouteau toward home. She didn't want to stay calm. She wanted a verbal "knock-down, drag-out" fight with no holds barred. She only hoped Dr. Fitzhugh was on night duty. Otherwise he just might have to miss a little sleep.

Chapter 34

*W*hen Kathy saw the van headlights flash across the room as Ed parked in the drive, she glanced at the huge old wall clock above the sofa. It read eleven-forty-five. She sat in the overstuffed brown chair directly across from the front door. She'd turned the lights off, seeing no need to burn them as she sat and seethed.

Ed unlocked the door, wheeled himself in, and flicked the light switch.

"Kathy! What are you doing sitting in the dark? You scared me half to death."

"I'm waiting for you," she said, barely able to keep her tone civil. "Where were you?"

"I told you, I had a client dinner tonight. We ran into some trouble."

She knew what that meant. He'd lost a bunch of money again. She wondered how much a "little trouble" amounted to this time.

"I tried to call. You weren't here. Where were you?"

His words caught her off guard. "I was at the hospital with Margaret. Micah had emergency surgery tonight."

Ed rolled aside so he could close the front door. "Is he okay?"

"He will be," Kathy said shortly. "His appendix burst, but he's doing okay." She didn't intend to dwell on this. She wanted her fight. She'd waited long enough.

"How much did you lose this time?" she asked.

"What?"

He looked totally confused, and Kathy glared at him. Her hands gripped the chair arms in an effort to control her rage. "Bruce told me you were at the Ameristar. You said you had some trouble. How much did you lose this time?"

Kathy didn't care when she saw the scowl on Ed's face, nor did it soften her when he pounded his fist on his chair arm and shouted. "It wasn't like that, Kathy."

"Then how was it?" she shot back. "Did your client grab your chair and force you into the casino? Did he make you play all this time? Bruce was home at eight o'clock, Ed."

Ed pushed himself to the middle of the room without a word. The silence grew long. Kathy waited. Experience had taught her that the person who spoke first usually lost. She didn't intend to lose any more than she already had. She didn't know how much money Ed had lost, but even if it was everything they owned, that couldn't begin to compare to how bereft she felt over her loss of respect for her husband. How dare he betray that trust, not once, but twice?

After what seemed long moments, but in fact was probably only seconds, Ed snapped, "So you found it necessary to check up on me? You didn't trust me to keep my word."

Kathy recognized the offensive attack to deflect her position. "No, Ed. I didn't check up on you until I needed to contact you. I needed to let you know where the kids and I were, and you weren't where you were supposed to be. Bruce said you left the restaurant together, and he was home by eight."

She paused for breath.

Ed glared at her. "I told you we had some trouble."

Kathy wasn't finished. "Who's we? Bruce got home just fine, and I came looking for you, Ed. I was afraid you'd been in a wreck, or the van had broken down. You were still at the casino at ten-thirty. I saw the van with my own eyes."

Ed shook his head. "You couldn't have, Kathy. The wrecker picked up Simpson's car at ten-fifteen, and as soon as he went inside and called his wife, we left. I drove him to Olathe and came straight home."

Kathy stared at Ed. What was he talking about? It didn't make sense, although she did remember seeing the tow truck with that black car.

Maybe—no.

Ed could have seen the truck, too, and made it fit his story. She wasn't that gullible. "Yes, and I'm Miss America," she snapped. She couldn't remember when ever she'd been this hurt and angry.

"No," Ed said. "Kathy, you have to believe me. Bruce and I tried to get Simpson to go to the Hereford House, but he insisted he wanted to go to the steakhouse at the Ameristar, so that's where we went. When we finished, Bruce was in the first parking lot, but Simpson and I were in the garage."

"So," Kathy interrupted, "after you dumped Bruce, you and Simpson went back in for a little fun."

"No!" Ed shouted. "No. We didn't go back in. When we got to the cars all four of Simpson's tires had been slashed. He couldn't drive his car, and it couldn't be towed. At that time of night we had a hard time finding a flatbed wrecker, and I couldn't leave him stranded. I tried to call you, and there was no answer. As soon as the wrecker came, Simpson called his wife. She was going to come and get him, but she said she had little kids in bed, so I told him I'd take him home. I tried to call you all evening."

Kathy blinked back the tears that threatened to spill down her face. She would not cry. She would not let Ed see that weakness in her. Was he telling the truth? It would be easy enough to verify tomorrow. All she had to do was call Bruce and ask. He would be in contact with Mr. Simpson in the morning. An afternoon call would prove or disprove Ed's story.

Kathy's mind whirled. As angry as she was, she recognized how crucial her response at this moment was to her marriage. Either she could trust Ed, or she could not. If she could not, how could she and Ed go on? Divorce was out of the question, but she knew she wouldn't be able to continue to live with a man she didn't trust. Legal separation sounded nasty to her, and yet she couldn't stand the thought of always wondering if she and the children would have a place to sleep and food to eat.

No, she had to decide here and now if she could trust this husband of hers.

"You didn't gamble—not even a few hands?" It shamed her to need to ask, but she had to. She had to have Ed tell her point blank, yes or no.

"No, Kathy, not even a few hands. I've told you what happened. The last time I tried to call you was between ten-fifteen and ten-thirty. After that I was on the highway to and from Olathe."

Kathy mentally replayed the evening. She knew she hadn't been home to receive any of Ed's calls, and she was so upset she hadn't checked the answering machine when she came in the second time. That much could be true, and she had seen that tow truck as she entered the Ameristar parking lot. That could have been Simpson's car. She tried to visualize the garage where she'd seen the van. There had been an empty spot next to the van. Simpson's car could have been parked there earlier, because she knew the garage filled quickly. That space wouldn't have been unoccupied for long.

Kathy struggled with the situation long moments. She wanted to believe Ed. She wanted her marriage to grow stronger, rather than crumble apart. She wanted them to trust one another.

Her anger slowly seeped away, and she knew she would not call Bruce tomorrow. She would trust Ed in this, and she would intensify her efforts to keep that trust healthy.

The first step came hard, though. Crow always went down rough.

"Ed, I'm sorry." She swallowed and began again. "I should have trusted you, but I was so worried. When I saw the van there so late—" She paused, but she knew she had to clean the slate. "I jumped to the wrong conclusion. I'm sorry."

She couldn't look at him, and her gaze on her hands offered no comfort either.

Ed rolled closer. "I guess I deserve that, Kathy, with my history, but I made a promise, and I thought you believed me."

"I did," Kathy wailed. "I did until I saw your van in the Ameristar parking lot long after you should have been home."

"You should have come inside and looked for me, or waited by the van. You couldn't have missed me by more than a few minutes."

"I was too upset," Kathy admitted. "I probably would have strangled you right there in front of God and everybody."

Ed laughed. He actually laughed. Kathy glanced up and caught his gaze before her mouth slit into a grin. In a moment, she, too, burst into a cascade of giggles.

"Come here," Ed said, his arms spread wide.

Kathy hesitated long moments. She could laugh now, but her fears had been overwhelming.

Ed rolled closer. "Kathy, I made a promise to you and to God. I'm not going to gamble again, ever." His eyes held a plea she couldn't deny.

She slid out of her chair and onto Ed's lap. "I was so afraid," she whispered into the nape of his neck.

"I know." He wrapped his arms around her and held her close. "I broke your trust once, Kathy, but I'll never do it again."

Kathy rested in her husband's arms and let his words comfort her. He hadn't broken his promise this time. In fact, he'd been doing a good deed. She'd worried over something that had a simple explanation. Shame washed over her. Ed had done his part, and now he needed a wife who believed in him, not one who doubted his every move.

She felt his hands stroke her back and feather along the nape of her neck. Moments ago his touch would have infuriated her even more than she already was. Now, knowing the truth, she melted into his embrace. Ed had been true to his word, and she resolved to be the trusting wife he deserved.

They held each other for long moments as a calm peace enfolded Kathy. Ed had lost the use of his legs, but he'd gained a stronger relationship with God, and with her. He'd made a few detours, but as Kathy thought about it, she realized even some of the apostles had a few bumps in their faith. Kathy snuggled deeper into Ed's arms. She had a good man. He'd made mistakes, but he'd overcome them, and now he was a better man than the one she'd married. She realized she was one of the most blessed women on earth.

Ed leaned back and looked deep into her eyes. "So, are we okay now?"

"Yes." Kathy sighed, secure in the knowledge that their relationship truly was steady. "Oh, yes," she replied as she rose and headed to their bedroom with a seductive glance over her shoulder. "We're much more than okay."

Epilogue

Six months later, Ed, Kathy, and the children entered the church vestibule where Micah greeted them.

"Good morning, folks. You're just the man I need to see," he told Ed.

"Well, here I am," Ed replied as he set the brakes on his chair.

"I got a call last night from the church in Overland Park," Micah said. "They've heard about your seminar about gambling, and they want you to come and do one for them. I gave them your number."

Ed shook a finger at the preacher. "You're going to have to quit that. I keep telling you I'm not a speaker, and you just keep getting me into these deals."

Micah laughed and turned to Kathy. "How can he say he's not a speaker when every time he does one of those seminars my phone rings off the hook with people asking how to book him at their congregation?"

"Beats me," Kathy said as she stooped and set Charis's carrier on the floor beside Ed. "He does this fantastic thing about gambling and how it can destroy your relationship with God and with your family. Maybe he's not a speaker, but he gets his point across."

Ed lifted Desmond to his knees. "All I can do is tell people how the best thing I ever did was sign up for the Bets Off program. Gambling can still be tempting, but I'd never again gamble my soul away, and a little insurance is not a bad thing. If that's all they want to hear, I can handle it."

Micah nodded. "Sounds like a speaker to me, and there are so many people who are hurting because of their weakness."

"Yes, and more than you realize spend years in therapy to break that addiction. I was blessed to get out when I did." Micah picked up Desmond and tickled him. "You wanted help, and Kathy was by your side to support you when you got weak."

"Maybe that's why people listen to me so well," Ed said. "I'm no speaker, but I know about weakness, and all I do is tell people about that, and what it almost did to me. Since I've been giving these talks I've met a lot of people who have lost their homes, their businesses, and their families. God was good to me when he gave me Kathy and my church family."

Micah nodded. "What amazes me is how people fell for the propaganda when the gambling bills were voted on. Most of the tax revenue has to be spent on additional police staff, and few ever hear about the people who are mugged or murdered on their way home after winning large amounts. Even I wouldn't know about that if I weren't on the city commission."

"I know," Ed agreed. "We all got a snow job. It's true there is a lot of tourist traffic pulled to the city, but the casinos get the lion's share of that business. Small businesses struggle to hire help, because a lot of the low scale work force went to the casinos. Even the promise of school funding got waylaid. Most of the money goes into the general funds, and the schools see very little of it."

Micah put Desmond down. "It is so sad to watch all that."

Kathy took her son's hand to lead him to class. Ed watched them walk down the hall before he turned back to Micah. "I almost gambled away my very most precious possessions. It's not hard to talk to people and try to convince them not to make that same mistake."

"Good," Micah said through a sly little grin. "Overland Park wants you next weekend."